Her chest filled with longing.

What would it be like if this were a family scenario, if they were Mom and Dad and kids, stopping for takeout on the way home from work?

Luke climbed into her small car, juggling the large, flat box to make it fit without encroaching on the gearshift.

Hannah had to laugh at the size of his meal. "Hungry?"

"Are you?" He opened the box a little, and the rich, garlicky fragrance of Pasquale's special sauce filled the car.

Her stomach growled loudly.

"Pee-zah!" Addie shouted from the back seat.

"Peez!" Emmy added, almost as loud.

"That's just cruel," she said as she pulled the car back onto the road and steered toward Luke's place. "You're tempting us. I may have to order some when I get these girls home."

"No, you won't," he said. "This is for all of us. The least I can do is feed you after you drove me around."

Her stomach gave a little leap, and not just at the prospect of pizza. Why was he inviting her to have dinner with him? Was there an ulterior motive? And if there was, would she mind?

Lee Tobin McClain is the *New York Times* bestselling author of emotional small-town romances featuring flawed characters who find healing through friendship, faith and family. Lee grew up in Ohio and now lives in Western Pennsylvania, where she enjoys hiking with her goofy goldendoodle, visiting writer friends and admiring her daughter's mastery of the latest TikTok dances. Learn more about her books at www.leetobinmcclain.com.

Books by Lee Tobin McClain

Love Inspired

Rescue Haven

The Secret Christmas Child
Child on His Doorstep
Finding a Christmas Home

Redemption Ranch

The Soldier's Redemption
The Twins' Family Christmas
The Nanny's Secret Baby

Rescue River

Engaged to the Single Mom
His Secret Child
Small-Town Nanny
The Soldier and the Single Mom
The Soldier's Secret Child
A Family for Easter

Visit the Author Profile page at Harlequin.com for more titles.

Finding a Christmas Home

Lee Tobin McClain

LOVE INSPIRED

INSPIRATIONAL ROMANCE

LOVE INSPIRED®
INSPIRATIONAL ROMANCE

ISBN-13: 978-1-335-56726-0

Finding a Christmas Home

This edition published by arrangement with Harlequin Books S.A.

For questions and comments about the quality of this book, please contact us at CustomerService@Harlequin.com.

Love Inspired
22 Adelaide St. West, 40th Floor
Toronto, Ontario M5H 4E3, Canada
www.Harlequin.com

Printed in U.S.A.

Behold, I make all things new.
—*Revelation* 21:5

To my Wednesday morning writers' group:
your helpful suggestions, positive energy and
sense of fun worked wonders on this book,
even in the midst of a pandemic.
I'm blessed to have you in my life.

Chapter One

Hannah Antonicelli walked out of the Rescue Haven Learn-and-Play and flopped down on the bench that ran along the wall of the red barn.

"Cold for sitting outside, isn't it?" Her friend Gabby wrapped her heavy parka more tightly around herself before sitting beside Hannah. Despite the fact that she and her husband oversaw all Rescue Haven's programs—the dog rescue, the after-school program for at-risk boys and the childcare center—Gabby always had time to stop and chat.

And Gabby was right: November in rural Ohio wasn't sit-outside weather. Wind whisked across the neighboring cornfields, rustling the dry, light brown stalks, carrying with it the faint, clean smell of oncoming snow. "I just need a minute before I start with the dogs," Hannah said.

"Take a minute! Take an hour, or the whole morning off, if you need. It's a great thing you're doing, providing a home for Marnie's girls."

"The Learn-and-Play is the only possible way I'll manage, so thank you for accepting the twins on short notice." And she didn't want to take advantage of Gabby's generosity by skimping on her part-time job as the Rescue Haven dog trainer. What with everything that had happened, she'd already taken too much time off. Not to mention the fact that Gabby was pregnant and didn't need extra stress. "Let me know if they need anything or get upset."

Caring for her sister's eighteen-month-old twin girls had been the right thing to do when Marnie had died of complications after a drug overdose two weeks ago. The desperate phone call from her estranged older sister had shaken Hannah's world at its foundation. She and Mom had rushed to Marnie's side and instantly agreed to care for the twins they barely knew.

Which meant that, for now, Hannah was back in her childhood home. Mom's house had plenty of space, a big yard with a tire swing and was close to Rescue Haven.

Anyway, until they got the twins' lives in order and their schedules figured out, it was going to take two of them to manage things. Being in the same house was just easier.

Mom was busy trying to keep her struggling bakery afloat during hard times. She was also grief-stricken and guilt-ridden over Marnie's death—not in any shape to be a primary caregiver. Whereas Hannah... Hannah was more angry at her sister than anything else. Marnie had neglected her babies. She'd caused terrible pain to their mother. And she'd entrusted Hannah with a secret that wasn't going to be easy to keep.

The blond, curly-haired twins had instantly become Hannah's priority in life. She had to raise them right, and she would. She yawned. The twins hadn't slept well last night—again—and she was just so tired...

She might have actually dozed off for a few seconds, and when she opened her eyes, she felt like she was dreaming. "Who's *that*?" she asked Gabby as she stared at the movie-star-handsome, rugged man striding toward them.

"You don't recognize him? That's Luke Hutchenson."

Hannah's stomach lurched. "When did he come back to town?"

"Gabby, we need you!" The voice from inside the Learn-and-Play was a little frantic, and the sound of a child crying, then another—neither of them the twins, thankfully—galvanized Gabby into action. "He'll tell you," she said, waving to Luke and then rushing into the building.

"Hey, Luke," Hannah said faintly as the man approached. She still felt a little like she was in a dream.

He tilted his head to one side, and then a slow smile crossed his face. "Hannah Antonicelli?"

That smile. Wow. She nodded and stood, hoping to keep their conversation short. And focused on him. "I haven't seen you for ages." Should she shake his hand? She brushed her palm down her jeans and then, when he didn't initiate a handshake, shoved it in her back pocket. No one else in the universe was as awkward with men as she was.

Well, men she found attractive, anyway.

And why was she finding Luke attractive? He was ten years older than her, or close. And the things she knew about his family could fill a soap-opera script. Of course, that meant he was out of reach, which was the kind of man she generally favored. "Um, are you in town for a visit?"

"Of sorts." He looked out across the fields for a minute, then met her eyes. "Dad's sick. Needs some pretty serious surgery, and there's no one but me to take care of him, since Bobby…"

She stared, waiting. Had something more happened to Bobby?

Bobby. A big flirt, cute and fun. Always in trouble, and now, in jail for second-degree murder.

Bobby, the twins' father. And no one could ever know.

Luke cleared his throat. "You might not have heard, but Bobby's incarcerated."

"I, uh, I did hear." And she hadn't really thought about how that would feel to his family, but now, seeing Luke's clenched jaw, she realized how painful Bobby's situation must be to him. Bobby had been part of a convenience-store robbery that had resulted in a killing. From what she'd heard, he'd gotten belligerent and refused a plea bargain, so there was no telling when he'd get out.

She touched Luke's arm. "I'm sorry. That must be tough."

"Yeah." He nodded. "Thanks. So how about you? What are you doing at Rescue Haven?"

It was an obvious move to change the subject, which was fine with Hannah, mostly. "I'm the dog trainer here," she said. "I have other clients, too, but Rescue Haven takes up more and more of my time. They're expanding, taking in more dogs."

"You always did love animals," he said. "I remember you playing with Old Man Richie's barn kittens."

His words brought back a flash of memory.

She'd been young, probably six, and she'd tagged after Marnie to Mr. Richie's barn. Marnie and her friends had promptly climbed up to the hay-loft to smoke cigarettes, leaving Hannah to the glorious bounty of a half-dozen kittens, no more than a week old.

Luke and Mr. Richie had burst into the barn at the same time. Mr. Richie had seen her just as he'd smelled the cigarette smoke, and he'd yelled in a scary way, talking about setting fires and burning down barns and destroying people's livelihoods. Hannah had backed against the wall and cried.

Luke had taken her hand and led her outside, given her an old bandana to dry her tears and reassured her that Mr. Richie wasn't yelling at her. Sure enough, the old man had emerged from the barn pushing Marnie, Luke's brother, Bobby, and their other two friends in front of him.

"I probably never said thank you back then, so thanks for saving me from Mr. Richie's wrath."

He snorted. "My brother could have used more of Mr. Richie's kind of direction, but he didn't get it."

"Marnie, too. Mom tried her best, but she worked long hours, and Marnie took advantage."

"How's Marnie doing?"

Hannah sucked in a breath. Most people in town had heard, via the usual gossip circuit, so she hadn't been faced with telling people very often. "She actually, um, she passed away. Very recently." Her throat tightened, but she swallowed her emotions. Marnie didn't deserve her sadness. "Of a drug overdose," she said firmly.

"You're kidding." His eyebrows drew together and he shook his head. "I'm sorry for your loss, Hannah. Awful, the toll drugs can take. How's your mom doing?"

"Not well." She hesitated, debating how much to tell him.

"I'm sure. It's not right, a child dying before a parent."

"Mom's really struggling." Hannah would have to tell him about Addie and Emmy, especially if he was going to be in town for a couple of weeks. There was no way he wouldn't hear, and it would seem weird that she hadn't mentioned them up front. "Marnie, um, she had twins. So Mom and I are taking care of them."

"How old?"

"Eighteen months." She nodded sideways toward the Learn-and-Play's entrance. "Gabby was good enough to accept them at the childcare here, so I can be nearby." Even just mentioning the girls sent a warm surge of love through Hannah's chest. She had to raise them well. Had to help them overcome the neglect they'd suffered as her sister had gone downhill.

"Is there a father in the picture?" he asked.

That was a normal question, she told herself as her face, neck and ears went impossibly hot.

And, as much as she didn't want to admit it, Marnie had been right about keeping the identity of the twins' father a secret. "No, there isn't," she said, and then made a show of checking the time on her phone. "I'd better get to work. Those dogs won't train themselves."

She turned toward the barn where the rescue dogs were housed, opening her mouth to say goodbye to Luke.

To her surprise, he fell into step beside her. "Let me know if there's anything you need for the dogs."

That was a weird thing for him to say, and for the first time she wondered what he was doing at Rescue Haven. Whatever his errand, she wished he'd finish it up and go away. She lifted her face to the cold breeze and looked up at the low-hanging clouds. Luke had always been popular—good-looking and the type of slightly bad boy all the girls flocked after. The type that awkward, shy girls like Hannah could only ever admire from afar.

"So, how long are you in town?" she asked. "Any plans for your time here?"

"Reese has some special projects in the works.

Their part-time handyman retired, so I'm working here for a couple of months."

"Oh, wow." Hannah gulped. They'd both be working at Rescue Haven. "Well, I should go check on the dogs."

She scurried away awkwardly, like a frightened mouse. But she *was* frightened. Because two months was a long time to keep a secret.

Luke started back toward the supply shed, trying to remember what he'd been doing before he'd run into Hannah.

He'd always liked cute little Hannah—who'd grown up to be way more than cute—but it seemed she didn't return the feeling. She'd sure acted strange when he'd said he worked here.

A police car pulled into the Rescue Haven driveway, spewing gravel. Luke's heartbeat escalated, then settled down, as he turned to see what was going on.

Between his father and brother, cops had been a regular part of Luke's childhood, and their appearance back then had never been a good thing. But he was a law-abiding citizen and an adult. He had no reason to feel guilty around the police.

The officer emerged, then opened the rear door and said something to the person inside. He reached in to help whoever it was.

Luke's father climbed out, batting away the

officer's hand even though he obviously could have used the support; it took him a couple of tries to get himself upright.

Luke's jaw tightened. What had Dad done now? At least Hannah had gone inside and wouldn't witness this.

He strode toward the cop and his father.

Dad was holding on to the roof of the car while the officer reached inside and then emerged with Dad's tall wooden cane. As Luke reached him, he smelled the whiskey emanating from his dad's breath. He jammed his hands in his pockets to keep himself from strangling the man. "Are you kidding me, Pop? Drinking at nine a.m.?"

"Hey, Luke," the officer said, holding out a hand. "John Pearson. I was a couple grades behind you in school."

"I remember you." Distractedly, Luke shook the man's hand.

"Saw your dad was having some trouble walking. It's a cold day. Heard you were working here, so I gave him a ride."

Luke's father muttered a few phrases under his breath. Something about how he hadn't needed the help—that he was fine—and the cops had no right to interfere. The whole mumbled speech was laced with profanity.

Anger swelled up in Luke and he glared at his father. "What were you thinking? You're having surgery right after Thanksgiving! On your liver!" He tried to lower his too-loud voice. "John gave you a ride. Which you needed. Can it."

Both his father and the police officer were looking at something behind him. He glanced over his shoulder.

There was Hannah, and from the way her forehead creased, she'd heard him scolding his father. She was probably close enough to smell the whiskey, too. He cringed inwardly.

"Thanks," he said to John. "I'll take it from here."

"Great." John looked relieved as he climbed back into his cruiser.

Luke helped his father over to the bench, swinging a wide berth around Hannah in the hope that she wouldn't hear Dad's profane grumbling. "Sit down a minute, Dad, while I settle a few things. Then I'll run you home."

Worries rolled around in his head. His father had said he wasn't drinking much anymore, per doctor's orders, and in the few days Luke had been in town, Dad had stayed sober. So what had caused him to fall off the wagon this early in the morning? Was he safe to be left at home alone, or did Luke need to take off the rest of the day—from the job he'd just gotten—in order to babysit him? Since Dad's liver problems were alcohol-related, what had this little binge done to his health?

Luke's chest rose and fell with rapid breaths, and he tried to slow down and think. He knew that being here to help his dad prepare for and then recover from surgery was the right thing to do, the Christian thing. But it wasn't going to be easy. And Dad wasn't going to be grateful.

"Everything okay?" It was Reese Markowski, the man who, along with his wife, Gabby, over-saw the Rescue Haven program. Reese focused primarily on the at-risk boys who came here after school to help train dogs. He was standing beside Hannah.

"Yeah," Luke said, shoving down his shame. "I just need to get Dad home."

"Take all the time you need," Reese said. "Our workload's going to escalate soon—I'm ironing out the details for a new project—but for now, nothing's an emergency."

"Thanks." Luke just wished this hadn't hap-pened in front of Reese and Hannah, both good people from good families, at least compared to his own.

"Is there anything I can do?" Hannah asked.

You can get out of here before you hear any-thing else that a lady shouldn't. "Thanks, we're fine," he said, knowing his voice was too curt for politeness.

If things were different, he'd have liked to spend more time with someone like Hannah, who was fresh-faced and hardworking, sweet. The polar opposite of the kind of woman he used to like.

But he couldn't escape his family, as evidenced by his father's appearance here today. He could never have someone like Hannah. Even if she was interested, he couldn't subject her to the trouble and foul language and rumors that went along with being a Hutchenson.

"Hey, I know you." Luke's father narrowed his eyes at Hannah.

Great. What now?

A few flurries of snow fell from the sky, and Hannah shivered. "Hi, Mr. Hutchenson," she said politely. "We're kind of neighbors," she said to Luke.

"Your mom still lives in the white brick place?"

She nodded. "Me, too, for now. Makes it easier to take care of the twins. Which means…" She trailed off.

"I'm your neighbor, too." Luke blew out a sigh. Between driving Dad to his appointments and getting this job, Luke had barely had a chance to look around him. He hadn't realized the Antonicellis still lived in the house just down the road. Close, if you didn't mind cutting through the trees or walking a country road, where cars tended to push the speed limit.

"Your mom doesn't like my dog," Dad said now to Hannah.

Hannah nodded. "I heard. Did you get the fence fixed yet?"

"I ain't fixin'—"

"I'll take care of it," Luke interrupted. His father's pit-bull mix looked intimidating and could act wild, but she was sweet-natured from what Luke could tell. She just didn't get enough attention. "Come on, Pop. I'll run you home and fix you a sandwich and coffee."

"Don't need to take care of me like I'm an invalid," Dad complained, but he did turn in the direction of Luke's truck.

"Nutrition is important," Luke told him. "Especially before surgery." It was also important to avoid alcohol, but that was a conversation better left for when his father was sober.

After Luke had basically lifted his father into the truck, he looked back toward Hannah, who stood talking to Reese.

So she'd learned that nothing in the Hutchenson family had changed. Plus, it looked like there'd be no escaping each other, since they were apparently neighbors as well as coworkers.

Luke just hoped that didn't turn out to be a disaster.

* * *

At the end of the day, Hannah hurried into the Learn-and-Play to pick up the twins, intending to take them right home. But they sat contentedly on the floor with Hannah's nephew, Mikey, who was almost four. Apparently, the other daycare kids had already been picked up.

Hannah's cousin Samantha waved Hannah toward the front of the room. "Sit a minute. We could both use a breather." Samantha was seven months pregnant, which had to make running the Learn-and-Play extra challenging, especially when she was mom to high-energy Mikey, as well.

"That's for sure." Hannah pulled a small chair over and perched on it beside Samantha, who'd claimed the only adult-size chair in the room. "Did they do okay?" She'd stopped in to check on the girls twice, and each time Samantha and her assistant had reassured her, but she still worried. They'd lost their mother and their home just two weeks ago, and the months before that had been difficult, their care inconsistent.

"They did well. I can already see how outgoing Addie is. She warmed up to everyone right away."

"And Emmy didn't?" Anxiety clutched at Hannah's stomach.

"She did fine, considering it's her first day

in a new environment." Samantha stretched her arms upward, and then twisted from side to side, her hands going to her back. "She's just a little more reserved."

"Did she cry much?"

"Some." Samantha tipped her flattened hand from side to side. "She cried more than Addie, but nothing unusual."

Still, Hannah worried. How was she going to manage if Emmy ended up needing more help and attention? She already felt stretched thin.

She watched the twins some more, and sure enough, Addie was waving her hands and laughing as Mikey made faces at her. Emmy watched quietly from a few feet away.

Samantha pulled a high chair close, sprayed disinfectant and wiped it down. "Mikey loves his cousins already. Second cousins, whatever. How could he help it? They're the cutest kids."

Hannah studied the twins. They had blond hair and blue eyes just as she and Marnie did, marking the fact that they'd descended from Northern Italians. While her own hair was relentlessly straight, though, Addie and Emmy had Marnie's adorable curls.

They didn't look a thing like their father, Luke's brother, who was dark-haired like Luke. For that, Hannah was grateful. Anything that would keep Luke from recognizing them as family members was a blessing.

And speaking of blessings, so was Hannah's cousin. "I'm so thankful for you," she said to Samantha. "I'm going to be hitting you up with a lot of newbie questions."

"Feel free, not that I'm any kind of expert," Samantha said. "I'm here for you. I can babysit or do playdates whenever you want."

Emmy burst into tears for no apparent reason, and Hannah hurried over to pick her up and comfort her. Addie reached her hands up, too, and Hannah plopped down onto the floor so that both twins could sit in her lap.

Samantha came over to where Hannah was sitting. "Come on, Mikey, let's get these toys picked up before Daddy comes," she said, and Mikey hurried to obey. "I can't wait for Corbin to take over for a few hours," she said to Hannah, keeping her voice low enough that Mikey couldn't hear. "I could use a nap."

"It would be great to have a man around," Hannah blurted, and then felt embarrassed, somehow exposed. "Just to help out with the twins," she added quickly.

"If you want a man around, you do have to go out on a date now and then," Samantha teased.

A weight settled on Hannah's heart. "Doesn't help in my case. Dates never go well."

"Ummm… I've been back in town for almost two years and I've never seen you go out on a date." Her cousin arched an eyebrow.

"I'm plain and unappealing. No one's ever going to give me a second look, let alone a second chance."

"That's ridiculous. You have no idea how pretty you are." Samantha reached out and fluffed a hand through Hannah's short, no-nonsense hair. "You might want to wear a little makeup and get your hair cut in a style," she suggested. "Not so much for a guy, but to give you confidence. Maybe wear a cute dress to church, instead of your same old jeans."

"Thanks a lot." But Hannah knew Samantha was right. She should make an effort no matter how discouraged she felt about her prospects of meeting anyone. "Meanwhile, it's just me and Mom to raise these two. I hope we're up for the challenge."

"And me!" Samantha mock-glared at her. "I'm your cousin. I'll help with your sisters' babies however I can. They're related to me, too." She pivoted and looked at the clock on the wall. "Come on, Corbin, where are you?"

As if responding to her call, Samantha's husband, a tall man dressed in rumpled khakis, with glasses perched crookedly atop his head, hurried in. "Sorry I'm late! I picked up a pizza so we don't have to cook."

"You're my hero." Samantha wrapped her arms around him for a long hug.

"Pizza!" Mikey ran at the couple and crashed into their legs, wrapping his arms around them. "Let's go home! I'm hungry!"

"Okay, okay." Corbin laughed, found Mikey's coat on a wall hook and kneeled to help the boy put it on.

Hannah stood. Time to follow suit. She needed to get the girls home before both they and she crashed. "Come on, kiddos, let's walk out with Mikey!" She grabbed the girls' jackets—pink for Addie, purple for Emmy—and brought them to where they were playing. She held up Addie's jacket. "Here, poke your arm in."

"No." Addie twisted away and headed for the toy bin.

Emmy, who'd been waiting her turn, got to her feet and followed her sister.

Hannah hurried after them with their jackets. "Come on, let's—let's both put one arm in, then the other." She took Addie's hand, but gently. She hadn't been around kids that much, but she did know that she had to figure out a way to distract them, rather than forcing them. Especially when there was a pair of them; no way could she pick up *two* screaming toddlers and carry them out, so she couldn't let things escalate that far.

"Uh-uh." Addie jerked away.

Emmy started to cry again.

Hannah looked at Corbin, Mikey and Samantha, all near the doorway, ready to leave but waiting. *Don't leave me alone with them!* she wanted to beg, but, of course, she didn't. "I'm sorry. I know you want to get home. I can lock up."

"No way. We won't abandon you." Corbin came over and kneeled in front of the girls. "Mikey is wearing his jacket. Can you put on your jacket like a big kid?" He spoke only to Emmy, probably having discerned she was the weaker link in the defiance chain.

Her eyes went wide and round.

"Like this, Emmy!" Mikey came over, pulled off his jacket and held it up. "See? I can put it on myself, 'cause I'm big." He demonstrated, sliding his arms into his jacket sleeves.

Please let this work, because I'm tired and starving, and I know they are, too.

Addie pushed her way in front of Emmy and thrust her arms into the jacket Hannah was holding. Samantha hurried over and held Emmy's jacket. "Put it on like Mikey," she encouraged, and praise the Lord, Emmy did.

"Let's all go home!" Samantha's voice was

singsong and she clapped her hands, and just like that, the twins followed her outside.

Hannah blew out a breath. "I have a lot to learn," she said as she grabbed the diaper bag and hurried after them.

Chapter Two

On Sunday morning, Luke sat in his hometown church—for the first time in his life—and fought the feeling that he didn't belong.

He'd done his best: he'd worn his good jeans and a button-down shirt, he'd smiled, he'd greeted people he knew, mostly his friendly new coworkers from Rescue Haven. The minister had shaken his hand and sounded sincerely glad, not just job-description glad, that Luke was here. Luke had even seen Hannah, hurrying toward the nursery with the twins right before the service started, and she'd given him a friendly wave.

But he'd caught the surprised looks, too. As kids, he and Bobby and their dad had never darkened the doors of any church. "Bunch of uptight hypocrites" was the kindest thing Dad had to say about Christians.

That was what Luke had believed, too, right

up until five years ago. A bad breakup, a job loss and an eviction had thrown him onto the streets. After a couple of months raising Cain right here in Bethlehem Springs, he'd gone back to Cleveland and landed in the humble, concrete-block building known as the Cleveland Christian Covenant men's shelter. The people there hadn't been uptight, or hypocrites; they'd fed him and helped him find an apartment and a paying job without once looking down on him. They'd offered church services and bible studies, but left it up to their clients, as they called the shelter's residents, whether to partake.

Luke had decided to try their brand of Christianity, and it had helped him start to heal.

Coming to church in his small hometown was different, but it shouldn't have been. He focused his mind on the Scripture readings and then prayed with the rest of the congregation. He listened to a sermon that made him think.

After services were over, as he headed to his car in a sharp wind, he saw Hannah walking ahead of him, holding a twin by each hand. She wore faded jeans and her parka was unzipped, her hair blowing haphazardly. Just looking at her made him smile. She was consistent, at least. And she didn't need to doll herself up; she was naturally pretty.

Which he shouldn't be thinking about. He sped up, reached his car and got in.

He was about to close the door when he heard a loud wail, then a muffled exclamation. He got back out and looked toward the corner of the parking lot from where the crying was coming.

Hannah was trying to get the twins into their car seats, but they weren't cooperating. Every time she leaned into the car, presumably to fasten one of them in, the other toddled away across the parking lot and Hannah had to abandon the mission to get the straying one to safety. One of the girls was loud about her unhappiness.

He debated with himself for a few seconds and then walked over. "Need a hand?" he asked her. "I can keep one corralled while you buckle in the other one."

"Thank you," she said, sounding frazzled. "That would help."

He squatted down to the level of the higher-energy toddler. "Are you gonna ride in the car?" he asked her, effectively blocking her from running across the parking lot.

"Car." She pointed at it. "No car."

So she was at the stage of learning words, probably dozens each week, which gave him an idea. "Where's your hat?" he asked.

"No hat," she said, and pulled it off.

Oh, well, bad idea. "Where's your nose?" he

asked, and they played a name-the-object game until Hannah was ready to get her into the car.

"No car," the child said, but her voice was tentative, and Hannah was able to pick her up and plunk her in her car seat with a minimum of drama.

She closed the back door and leaned against it, forking her fingers through her hair. Despite the chilly wind, she looked hot. "Thank you," she said.

"No problem. They're really cute." He looked into the window and tapped on it, making Addie laugh.

Just in that minute he'd looked away, Hannah's face had shifted from friendly to tense. "Right," she said, and walked around to the driver's side. "I should get going."

Luke watched her, puzzled. Had he said something wrong? Or was it that she didn't like him talking to her kids?

"Well, Luke Hutchenson! You're the last person I'd expect to see in church."

He turned to see a silver-haired woman in a fur coat. Her face was familiar, but he didn't remember her name.

No matter. She knew his.

Everyone knew his. If his family's reputation hadn't been bad enough, Luke's own carousing months in town just before he'd hit bottom had surely helped to cement it.

The older woman approached the car. "Are these poor Marnie's twins?" she asked, peering into the back seat.

"Uh-huh. See you later." Hannah climbed into the car, but not before Luke registered her tightened lips and tense face. She backed out, a little too fast, and drove away.

A silver Lincoln Continental pulled up, and the driver-side window opened. "I've been looking all over for you!" said the driver, sounding irritated.

The fur-coat woman looked at her watch and then hurried to the passenger side, muttering about how someone should open the door for her.

Luke wondered if she meant for him to do it. Really?

But before Luke could move, Reese, his boss at Rescue Haven, was there. He opened the door for the woman, who Luke now remembered as Marla Evans. Reese said a few words to her, closed her safely into the big luxury car and watched it drive away. Then he turned to Luke. "Hey, man, saw you helping Hannah with the twins. Looks like you have a knack for it."

"I like kids," Luke admitted. "Especially at that age. They're a hoot." He forced his throat to relax, trying to sound casual. There was no real reason for the loss of Nicolette to be so painful to him, still.

Yet once his mind went in that direction, it was hard to stop. How old would she be now... seven? Eight? Where was she living?

Reese was looking at him funny. "Do you have any children?"

"No." He looked away from Reese's curious stare. He could've been a dad to Nicki, but he'd screwed up.

"Hannah's real pretty," Reese said.

Luke jerked his head around and glared at the man.

Reese arched an eyebrow. "She seems lonely, too. Maybe you should ask her out."

That thought appealed in too many ways. But he wouldn't want to let another kid, or kids, down. "Nah. I'm no good for her."

Reese narrowed his eyes, still studying Luke. "You heard the sermon, right?"

"Right." It had been about being washed clean, a new creation.

Reese opened his mouth like he was going to say more, but Gabby came out of the church, holding her two-year-old daughter, Izzy, by the hand, and waved at them.

"Gotta go," Reese said. "She's getting tired easily these days."

Gabby didn't look tired in the least, but Luke

wasn't going to argue. He just waved as Reese hurried to his family. Then he turned and headed to his own car.

By the time he reached it, the parking lot was nearly empty. Just like another parking lot on that long-ago afternoon, when he'd stood waving at Nicki as her angry mother drove her away.

Back then, he'd gotten in his car and bawled like a fool, and not for the end of the relationship, which had been going downhill for months. Instead, his grief had been for the fact that he'd never get to watch that sweet child wake up in the morning again, that he'd never read her another bedtime story, that he'd miss her first day of kindergarten and every other first in her life.

Nicki hadn't understood, when she'd blown him kisses and waved goodbye, that she'd never see Luke again, but she must have figured it out later. Had she been sad? Wondered what had happened to the man she'd called Da-da from the time she'd learned to talk?

One thing was for sure, Nicki would never hear a good word about him from her mother, and understandably so. He'd been a jerk of a boyfriend.

Just like a Hutchenson.

Kids were precious, and they deserved better than the likes of him.

* * *

On Sunday afternoon, the breeze settled down enough that Hannah and her mother took the twins outside in the yard. The girls ran toward the outdoor playset, Addie ahead as always, Emmy following more slowly. Hannah had to admit, again, that living here at Mom's house was the best move for all of them. Hannah loved her own cozy home, but Mom had equipment from a brief stint doing home childcare years ago, and the girls loved being pushed in the little swings and climbing the ladder to the slide. It made Hannah happy to hear them shriek and giggle, and even Mom smiled more than she had since losing Marnie.

When the girls tired of climbing, Hannah pulled out a giant bottle of bubbles she'd gotten at the discount store and swung the wand to create a cascade. Emmy's eyes got round, and Addie immediately leaped to try to catch them.

Hannah *wasn't* going to think about how much they looked like her beautiful, troubled sister.

"Do you think they've done this before?" Mom asked, kneeling to show Emmy how to wait for a bubble to land on her hand.

Hannah shoved aside her sad thoughts of Marnie and pulled her usual angry attitude back to the forefront. "Doubtful, considering the kind of mom Marnie was."

"She tried," Mom said.

"Did she, though?"

"Of course, she did! She loved them. And we don't need to talk about this while they're listening."

"You're right. Sorry." Hannah waved the wand to produce more bubbles.

In her heart, she fumed. Mom always made excuses for Marnie, but the truth was, her sister had wanted nothing to do with either Mom or Hannah. Marnie had moved to Indianapolis two years ago—pregnant with the girls, unbeknownst to Hannah and her mother—and then she'd hidden the twins' existence for months. No, she didn't have time for a visit. She couldn't talk long. She wanted to make a fresh start and was doing fine.

Eventually, though, it became obvious that Marnie had gotten back onto the roller coaster of drug use. During a phase when she'd been dedicated to a twelve-step program, she'd reconciled with Mom and Hannah, and they'd driven out to see her.

She, Mom and Marnie had gotten along fine at first. Hannah and her mother had marveled over the babies, helped with them, taken a lot of pictures. But then some perceived criticism of Marnie's lifestyle meant that she had kicked them out.

Hannah blew more bubbles. The wind swept them toward the tree line and Addie sped after them. Emmy ran, too, stumbled, then picked herself up and followed her sister.

"I don't know why Marnie always took offense at what I said." Mom perched on the picnic table and rested her elbows on her knees, her chin on clasped hands. "I sure wish I'd tried harder to reconnect."

"You did try." They'd talked about it so many times, but it seemed to make Mom feel better to return to the subject, over and over. "You called, and emailed, and texted. Way more than I did."

Every effort had ended in Marnie hanging up the phone in anger. Hannah had talked to their pastor about it and had learned about mental-health issues and how you sometimes just had to let someone hit bottom.

Unfortunately, Marnie had hit bottom so hard that she'd overdosed on a soup of street drugs and alcohol. Someone had dropped her off at an emergency room, and the hospital had notified Hannah and her mother as next of kin. They'd gotten on the road within an hour and driven like mad, arriving in time to talk with Marnie, individually and together, before she lost consciousness for the last time.

"I don't know what these little ones went through, as she was going downhill." Mom's voice was shaky, and when Addie ran close by her, she reached out, picked her up and gave her a fierce hug, letting her free as soon as she started to struggle. "That friend who was keeping them at the end... I don't know." Mom squeezed her eyes shut and shook her head.

"It wasn't a great environment, but they were safe." At least Marnie had done that much. And she'd regretted her failures; she'd sobbed to Hannah when they'd been alone together, confessing the way she'd neglected her daughters.

That hour alone together was when Marnie had extracted a promise from Hannah that she wouldn't reveal that the twins' father was a local convicted felon.

"More!" Addie hugged Hannah's leg and then pointed at the bubbles, and Hannah snapped back to the here and now, her adorable nieces and the weak, late-fall sunshine.

There was the sound of a car engine revving, then revving again, and black smoke was visible over the tree line from the Hutchensons' place. A dog barked loudly, over and over again. "Does Luke's dad bother you?" Hannah asked her mother, squinting through the bare trees to where the man's junk-filled driveway was barely visible.

"Not too much. He makes noise, and that dog of his got off its chain and ran through my flower beds last summer, but it's nothing I can't handle." Mom frowned. "He's struggling with what happened with Bobby. It's so hard when your child is in trouble and you can't help."

"Right." Hannah didn't dare say any more. Marnie hadn't told their mother that Bobby Hutchenson was the twins' father, and she'd made Hannah promise not to tell her, either.

Marnie hadn't wanted them to carry the stigma of an incarcerated father, and Hannah couldn't disagree with that. It wasn't as if Bobby could pay child support or had even acknowledged being their father. Hannah wasn't sure he even knew about the twins. Not for the first time, she wished there'd been time to talk to her sister about it more, to understand what had led to the connection and breakup, why Bobby had been uninvolved with his children and whether that really needed to go forward into the future.

The twins, oblivious to all the adult concerns, were still trying to catch the bubbles Hannah periodically blew.

"I hate to do this," Mom said, "but do you mind if I go in now? I need to put together the schedule for next week." As the sole proprietor of a busy bakery, Mom always had too much to do. The trip to Indianapolis and then getting the twins settled had meant that she'd left things in the hands of her manager, who'd only been able to do the bare minimum. Mom was still trying to catch up.

"That's fine," Hannah said. "I've got it covered." She'd known when they'd brought the twins home that the responsibility of caring for them would fall most heavily on her, and she was good with that. Only occasionally did she think, longingly, about how relaxing it would feel to go home to her own cozy house and read a book throughout a long, lazy Sunday afternoon.

Those days are gone. She sent another set of bubbles floating over the twins' heads and then put down the bottle and chased along with them, which made the twins shriek and laugh even more.

They were sweet, beautiful innocents, and Hannah was going to make up to them for what their mother had done.

From the Hutchensons' house, there was the sound of more loud barking and some shouting. Then, a large gold-colored pit bull burst out of the bushes separating their houses. The dog was headed straight for the twins.

Chapter Three

Luke didn't wait to see whether his father could control his dog. He just ran after the creature as fast as he'd ever run in his life. If something happened to one of those little girls because Luke hadn't gotten the fence repaired fast enough…

The delighted shrieking he'd heard before had taken a bad turn. Now, he could hear children's voices crying in fear.

He burst out of the bushes and ran across the big backyard, arms and legs pumping, heart pounding. Hannah was blocking the dog's access to the twins, jumping in front of it as it tried to dodge around her.

The twins were screaming and hiding behind her. She waved them away.

"Addie," she ordered, her voice loud enough that Luke could hear it, but still sounding calm, "hold Emmy's hand and walk inside to Grandma, nice and slow."

"I 'cared!" One of the girls started to run, and the other stumbled after her. Both were crying.

Luke sprinted as hard as he could. Almost there.

"Stop. Stay." Hannah's commands, pitched low, were directed at the dog.

The dog ignored the order. She thought chasing the twins would be a good game, apparently, and she dove past Hannah in the direction of the smaller, slower girl.

Hannah grabbed for the dog, catching her collar.

First one, then the other child headed back toward Hannah, coming too close to the exuberant dog, and Hannah lost her grip.

Luke plunged into the fray and swept the slower girl up in one arm, the quicker twin in the other. His heart pounded, and Goldie jumped at him, but at least the little girls were high in his arms, out of reach.

Hannah gave stern orders to the dog, orders the untrained creature had no idea how to obey, but the authority in her voice seemed to calm Goldie a little. The jumping slowed down. Problem was, every time one of the twins let out an ear-splitting scream—which was about every five seconds, and Luke's ears were right next to their mouths—the dog barked and jumped.

Luke's dad appeared with a frayed rope.

"She busted out again. You shouldn't have had these kids over here making all that noise." He caught the dog and leveled a hard hit against her head, and when she cowered, he looped the rope through her studded collar and tied it tight.

"Your mother's gonna be yellin' at me again," he said to Hannah. "Get her out here, and I'll explain."

"Let's leave Mom out of it." Hannah was breathing hard, but amazingly, her voice was steady. "She's having a tough time right now."

Actually, Luke could see, Hannah's mother was standing in the kitchen doorway, talking on her cell phone.

The twins settled a little in Luke's arms. The outgoing one stared at the dog and Luke's father, while the other gulped and wiped her eyes and reached for Hannah.

Dad jerked the dog's rope, making her yelp. "She's a noisy thing but she won't hurt anyone. She's just a year old, still a pup. Doesn't know any better."

She doesn't know any better because you didn't teach her better.

Sort of like Bobby. Sort of like Luke.

Hannah took the still-whimpering little girl from Luke. "Have you tried to work with her?"

"I got her one of those electric collars. She just won't listen." Dad tickled the chin of the little girl Luke still held in his arms, clicking his tongue, and the child actually laughed. Then Luke remembered his father loved babies and was good with them.

The sound of a police siren cut through the country stillness, and Luke got a bad feeling. Someone, maybe even Hannah's mom, must have heard the commotion and called the cops.

Sure enough, thirty seconds later, a cop pulled up in front of Hannah's house, lights flashing.

A moment later, John Pearson, the same officer who'd picked up Dad before, walked up the sidewalk and into the back yard, causing Goldie to bark frantically again. "This the dog that was loose?"

Dad was puffing up, defensive, so Luke spoke up. "She got away, but she's under control now."

Goldie lunged, this time at a passing squirrel, pulling the rope from Luke's father's hands. It was only Hannah's quick movement, as she stepped on the rope and then grabbed it, that prevented another escape.

Pearson tilted his head to one side, looking skeptical. "I'll have to issue a citation," he said. "Dogs are required to be on a leash."

Dad scowled. "Aw, come on—"

"And if she's gone after children, even playfully, then we need to take it seriously." He pulled out a form pad and a pen and started filling in the blanks.

"She's costing me money I don't have." Dad crossed his arms. "If I put her down, will you hold off on the citation?"

"Dad!" Luke couldn't believe his father would toss away an animal's life so carelessly.

The officer stopped writing. "You'd do that?"

Hannah's mouth had dropped open at Dad's words. "Don't put her down," she said now. "I'll work with her."

"*We'll* work with her," Luke said. "Together."

Even though Hannah felt for Goldie, who was wild but obviously sweet-natured, she put off training the dog as long as she could. Over the next couple of days, she sent information that Luke could share with his dad and suggested a few videos to watch.

He messaged her back that he was trying, but getting frustrated, and that his dad wasn't making any effort at all. Officer Pearson had stopped by to check on their progress, which was nonexistent. His dad was still talking about putting the dog down.

What could she say but "bring her over"?

Mom had the girls inside, helping her to bake cookies, though they were obviously more of a hindrance than a help. Darkness came so early these days, but Hannah had turned on the big floodlight to give them a space to work with. If all went well, they'd be able to work with Goldie at Rescue Haven, too.

More time with Luke. Yay.

The trouble was, a part of her *did* feel glad. She admired the way Luke had rushed in to save the girls and the nonblaming way he was willing to help train his father's dog. Watching him at Rescue Haven, she saw how hard he worked, how readily he smiled at the kids who attended programs there, how easily he lifted boxes and equipment.

She puffed out a breath, making a cloud in front of her, and rubbed her hands together. It wasn't snowing—not yet—but the ground was frozen and the bright stars foretold a temperature drop tonight.

"Hey, it's us." Luke's quiet voice was punctuated with a panting sound; Goldie was pulling hard at her leash, and only Luke's strength kept her from tugging him across the yard.

"Hey." She didn't look at Luke, but focused on the dog instead. As always, that helped. Goldie had the lanky look of an adolescent dog, some white markings on her muzzle and a big panting smile. "She's never been trained at all?"

"I don't think so. Dad's had her for a year or so, but he's mostly tied her up outside." He held up a hand. "I know, it's not the best. But he doesn't know any better. And I've been so busy with trying to find work and put Dad's house in order, Goldie slid down the list."

"Understandable." She reached into her pocket pouch and pulled out a treat. "Is she food-motivated?"

Goldie lunged for the treat, but Hannah held out a forearm, stopping the dog. "That answers that. So we'll work on taking treats nicely, and the 'sit' command."

"Sorry she's so rowdy. And that I have no clue about dog training."

"Don't worry about it. We're just experimenting." She kneeled in front of the slobbering, excited dog, feeling calmer and more collected as she entered her area of expertise. A dog was a puzzle, one she was good at solving.

She held out another treat. "Take it nice," she scolded, and closed her hand as Goldie lunged. She opened her hand again, and this time, the lunge was slighter, so she allowed the dog to have the treat.

"What kind of treats are those?" Luke asked, his nose wrinkling.

"Just little training treats." She held one up to him, smiling. "Want a taste?"

He took the treat, sniffed and wrinkled his nose. "Disgusting," he said, and handed the treat to the dog, who snapped her big jaws together for it. "Ow!"

"Okay—" Hannah stood up "—so that's your first lesson. Never give her a treat unless she takes it nice. Just close your hand over it." She demonstrated, and again on the second try, Goldie took the treat with a decent amount of gentleness.

"She's smart. That's good." She took another treat and held it above the dog's nose, then moved it up and back. As soon as the dog's haunches touched the ground, she gave her the treat. "See? That's how we'll teach her to sit."

After a couple of reps, which Luke watched closely, she held out a handful of treats to him. "Now you try it."

He lured the dog into position with the treat just as Hannah had done. "Yes!" he said when she sat.

Goldie sat tall, looking proud.

"See, she senses your approval and she likes it. Now, just do that same thing about a hundred times. Literally, over the next few days."

Luke repeated the steps, and as soon as his hand started to move, Goldie sank down onto her haunches. "Good girl!" he said, giving her the treat and then rubbing her head. "That's amazing!"

"She's smart, see?" Hannah loved this moment with new clients, when the owner figured out that their dog could learn, and the dog started enjoying positive attention.

"Thank you." He smiled up at her and Hannah felt the impact of it all the way to the tips of her toes.

She cleared her throat. "Okay, we'll just do a tiny bit of impulse control and then give her a break."

She lured Goldie into a sit, but instead of giving the treat, she took a minuscule step back, holding out her hand like a stop sign. After ten seconds, she let the dog have the treat.

Goldie swallowed it and sat, looking from Hannah to Luke and back again. "She wants more treats," Hannah said, laughing. "What a sweetie." She rubbed the dog's ears and sides, earning a sloppy kiss.

"Don't you give commands?" Luke asked.

"Only after the dog starts to learn a behavior," she said. "And speaking of learning, her brain's tired. Let's let her sniff around for a few minutes while we figure out some training goals."

"And a cost," he said. "We want to pay your going rate."

She looked up at him. "No need for that. I offered, and Goldie's our neighbor. You don't have to pay me."

"That's your livelihood," Luke said firmly. "We're paying."

And by that he meant that he was paying, because Hannah was pretty sure his father wasn't willing to invest in dog training. But Hannah had guessed, from the car Luke drove and his need to get a job quickly, that he didn't have a big savings account. He'd said he'd been able to drop everything and come help his father because he'd been working contract jobs in Cleveland. That probably meant he'd had periods of unemployment.

She'd let him pay, but a discounted rate.

"Woo-hoo!" Samantha came around the side of the house, setting Goldie off into a spree of barking. Samantha laughed and bent down to pet the dog's big head, then looked up at Hannah. "Hey, girl, have I got good news for you!" She glanced over at Luke. "Hi, Luke," she added, one of her eyebrows arching just a little as she glanced from Luke to Hannah.

Goldie jumped up toward Samantha and Luke pulled her back hard. "No jumping."

"We'll work on that," Hannah promised. Heat rose in Hannah's face, which was ridiculous. "I'm just training Luke's dog," she said without looking at Luke. "He and his dad hired me."

"Oh! So…"

"Right." She frowned at Samantha and stood up straight, trying to look all professional.

"So you two aren't—"

"No!" they both said at the same time.

Which, inexplicably, hurt Hannah's feelings. Was it so inconceivable that they'd be doing whatever Samantha had meant to imply they were doing? She gestured Samantha toward the porch steps.

Luke maintained a little distance as he squatted down beside Goldie.

"That's good, because… I set you up on a date!" Samantha sank onto the steps with some difficulty, grabbing Hannah's arm. "Good grief, I'm as big as a house. This baby is going to be huge."

"Why'd you set me up on a date?" Hannah's face burned hotter. Discussing her dating life, or lack thereof, was *not* something she wanted to do in front of Luke. "You know I hate that."

Here on the steps, they were outside the floodlight's radius, but a nearly full moon cast silvery light. Hannah put up her hood against the cold air, hoping to hide her blushing.

"Yeah, but, this is a really nice guy. Corbin's friend from out west. He does the same kind of research Corbin does." She looked over at Luke, who'd kneeled to rub Goldie's ears. "Animal science," she explained, even though Luke hadn't asked. "He's a professor, too. They're going to team up on something next summer."

"The one who wears a cowboy hat and boots?" Hannah had seen him around Rescue Haven.

"That's the one. He's some kind of genius, like Corbin, but he won't come on real strong. He's quiet. You'll have fun with him."

Hannah let out a disgusted snort. "Yeah, I'm sure." She sneaked a glance at Luke, who was watching their interchange with an impassive face.

"She never dates," Samantha said, for some reason feeling the need to explain. "But we— Gabby and I—think she should."

"Why don't you date?" Luke's voice sounded funny. Probably, he was trying not to laugh.

"Because I'm a loser with men," Hannah said. Might as well get that reality out into the open right away, as long as Samantha seemed set on revealing everything about her life to Luke.

"And the twins are going to need a man in their lives," Samantha said. "Not to mention that you'd be a great girlfriend, if you'd give guys a chance. So that's why I set you up with Dylan."

Hannah blew out a sigh. "I don't want—"

"It's just one date. He'll pick you up Friday at six. And I'm coming over to help you dress up, so you don't wear baggy jeans and a T-shirt."

"But—"

"Look, he's only in town for a couple of weeks here and there, until next summer, when he and Corbin will do a longer project together. So it's perfect for you. Low-key. Nothing intense. Good practice, at least." Samantha glanced at her phone. "Hey, look, I have to go. I was just driving by, and I thought, let me tell her in person so I can convince her." She smiled brilliantly, hugged Hannah, waved to Luke and headed back around the house to her car.

Hannah glanced at Luke and then away. "That was embarrassing."

"Why do you think you're a loser with men?" he asked, easing down into a sitting position.

Hannah leaned back on her elbows, shrugging. "I don't know." Even though she did. "I just don't like it. It's awkward. *I'm* awkward." Leave it at that.

"Dating's pretty easy." Luke grinned ruefully. "I've had a lot of practice."

"So I hear."

He looked at her quickly, his eyes flashing with something like hurt. Or maybe she'd imagined it.

"You were one of the most popular boys in high school, from what Marnie said," she explained quickly. "That's all I meant."

"High school." He waved a dismissive hand. "Being popular there is nothing to be proud of."

"I wouldn't know." She rubbed her hands together. It was cold, but she felt strangely comfortable. Now Luke knew most everything about her. There was nothing to hide.

Well, except for Marnie's secret.

"I can give you some pointers, if you want," he said.

"Pointers about what?"

"About dating."

She stared at him, unable to react to what he'd said. Luke Hutchenson—popular, handsome Luke Hutchenson—was offering to give her pointers about dating?

"Guy's point of view," he explained.

Her heart pounded, drumlike, as the reasons that would be a bad idea flashed through her mind, one after another.

She'd had only bad experiences with dating, and talking with Luke about it would bring all of them to the forefront. Maybe she'd even blurt out things that she shouldn't.

Luke was the twins' uncle, and she was bound to keep that secret.

And, maybe most of all, she was attracted to Luke, so listening to him wax eloquent about all his dating experience would just plain hurt.

"It's fine, I'll be fine," she said quickly, and soon made an excuse to go inside.

No need to get Luke involved in the disaster she'd almost certainly make of this upcoming date.

Friday night at five thirty, Luke stood on Hannah's doorstep, knocked and asked himself who he thought he was kidding.

He looked down at Goldie, who sat panting, almost smiling, beside him. She seemed to like Hannah, the lady with all the treats. At least, she'd been happy to come over tonight.

The door flew open, and there was Hannah, only it was Hannah like he'd never seen her before. Boots, tights, a skirt and sweater that showed... Wow. His mouth went dry. Hannah looked good. Really, really good.

"What? What are you doing here?" Hannah was fiddling with an earring. She sounded like she was ready to cry.

"I, um..." What *was* he doing here?

Goldie gave a bark of greeting, and Hannah's face creased into her usual smile. "Hi, girl!" She set the earring on an end table and opened the door, and when Goldie rushed in, she knelt down, quick and easy, and rubbed the dog's sides. It was clear why Goldie adored her already.

"I thought you might need some last-minute dating advice," he said. *Weak. That is a weak excuse for coming over when you know she has a date.*

She stood, her forehead wrinkling. "He's going to be here any minute!" She turned, walked across the living room and sat on the edge of the couch, patting her leg and clicking her tongue at Goldie, who trotted to her. "I'm a nervous wreck," she admitted as she stroked the dog's back.

Seeing as she hadn't kicked out Luke, maybe she wanted to talk. "Why are you so upset? It's just, what, a dinner date?"

She nodded miserably. "I was hoping we could go to Cleo's Café. In and over with fast. But turns out he's taking me to some Asian-fusion place up in Cleveland. I don't even know what Asian fusion is. I'll probably hate everything."

The guy was going all out. For a first date? "So you'll have about a forty-five-minute ride, and then dinner," he said.

"Right. It's way too much time, and what if he's, you know..." She trailed off. Sweat was breaking out on her forehead, little shiny drops.

"Boring? Handsy?"

"That," she said. She grabbed her phone and looked at it. "Is it too late to cancel?"

"Yeah. Unless you tell him you're sick when he gets here, but..."

"I couldn't do that. That's mean."

He studied her. She was dressed to impress, but her face was completely miserable. "Why'd you agree to go, anyway?"

"Addie and Emmy need a man," she said. "Oh, I know that sounds awful, but it's true. They need a father figure."

"Well…" He could see that, sort of, but starting from scratch with some guy she didn't even know seemed like a questionable approach. "Where are the twins?"

She blew out a breath. "Mom and Samantha decided they're too much, at first. So Mom took them over to play with her friend's grandchild." Still with the miserable expression on her face.

"Do you always do exactly what your mom and your friend say to do?"

She opened her mouth and then closed it again. Good. Maybe she'd rethink the whole date-to-get-the-twins-a-dad thing.

The doorbell rang.

Goldie went into her usual hysterics, barking wildly and leaping up at the door.

Luke grabbed the dog's leash and tugged her back. Hannah opened the door. Goldie continued barking and trying to lunge at the man on the other side of it. He was wearing a sport coat and khakis and smiling.

Who wouldn't smile, coming over for a date with a woman who looked like Hannah?

She opened the door. "Hi. Come in." As he did, she looked over her shoulder at Luke. *Go,* she mouthed to him.

In a flash, he made the comparison. Here he stood in his old jeans and sweater. He hadn't shaved this morning, and he knew his heavy stubble made him look disheveled.

And that was only the outside. Luke had a high-school diploma. This guy probably had a PhD, like Corbin.

As soon as Dylan entered, Goldie leaped up on him. "Sorry, sorry," Luke said, pulling her back. Only he wasn't sorry Goldie had gotten a little mud on the guy's coat.

"Take another step back," Hannah said in her dog-trainer voice. "Don't let her greet someone until she's calm."

"It's no problem," Dylan said easily, reaching down to rub Goldie's head. "Dogs are dogs."

Dylan seemed like an okay guy. Still, if he was planning to make a move on Hannah, as she'd worried... He shortened Goldie's leash and stuck out a hand. "Luke Hutchenson," he said in his deepest, least friendly voice.

"Dylan Smith." The man gave a firm handshake. The calluses weren't what Luke expected from a professor. Dylan looked curious about Luke's presence, but not intimidated. "Glad to meet you," he said.

"Luke is here because I'm helping to train Goldie, but we're done." Hannah glared at Luke. Apparently, she'd lost her nervousness about this date.

And why not? The guy seemed fine. Like a great prospect for her.

"I was just leaving. See you tomorrow." Luke let himself out the door, tugging a reluctant Goldie beside him.

Dylan Smith was everything Luke wasn't. And if Luke was any kind of good person, he needed to step aside, stay far away from Hannah and leave the two of them to build a relationship.

Chapter Four

Hannah usually enjoyed the camaraderie of Rescue Haven's Monday-morning staff meetings, which took place in the classroom area of the barn where the dogs were kenneled. But today, Gabby and Samantha sat side by side, deep into comparing notes on their rapidly advancing pregnancies. Reese was preoccupied with something on his tablet. And Luke was... Luke. He was leaning on a hay bale a little apart from the cluster of chairs where everyone else sat, looking straight ahead, his expression brooding.

He'd been at Rescue Haven for less than two weeks, and although everyone seemed to like him and think he was doing a good job, it wasn't surprising that he was a little aloof. Nothing Hannah needed to worry about.

Hannah sat down beside Gabby, and Reese

called the meeting to order, updating everyone on this week's schedule as a latecomer arrived: Hannah's Friday-night date, Dylan.

Luke muttered something under his breath, and Gabby nudged Hannah. "I want to hear about your date," she whispered.

Hannah nodded. She was surprised to see Dylan at the staff meeting, but since he was conducting some research on the dogs for the next few weeks, it made sense. She gave him a shy wave and he smiled back.

Their date had been nothing like she'd expected; it had been better, in a strange way.

A noise from outside set off the dogs, and they all started barking madly. Hannah hurried over to cover the crates of the three most agitated dogs. That would quiet them quickly, she knew, and then the dozen remaining dogs would settle down.

"Obviously," Reese said when the dogs' barking had quieted and Hannah was seated again, "having our staff meetings in the kennel isn't ideal. But that may be changing." He explained that Rescue Haven's two main donors, wealthy Mrs. Markowski—Reese's aunt—and the church, headed by prickly Mr. Romano, had come up with a challenge for the group.

There was a mixture of excitement and groans.

"Those two are always setting us ridiculous deadlines and making us prove ourselves," Gabby complained.

"But sometimes, it can work out well." That was Samantha, who'd had to prove her abilities working on a parade float, of all things, before being hired to start the Learn-and-Play program.

"I, for one, am grateful for the Learn-and-Play. That challenge was totally worth it." Hannah leaned back in her chair. "I don't know what I'd do if the twins couldn't attend a program right here where I work."

"Exactly." Reese smiled at her. "And you'll like this next opportunity, too, I think. Mr. Romano and my aunt have teamed up to offer us funds to renovate the old storage barn into a new dog-training facility. They're hoping we can use it for the dogs here, plus bring in paying customers from town who'll help fund our programs. And, as a bonus, we'd get more townspeople interested in Rescue Haven. And have more space for our meetings."

"That's brilliant!" Samantha pumped a fist in the air. "Just what we need to extend our reach."

Hannah wrapped her arms around herself, her heart pounding with excitement. "That would be amazing. A real, up-to-date training facility…" It was more than she'd ever dreamed of having in a small town like Bethlehem Springs. "We could do agility classes, scent work… It would be great for the rescue dogs as well as the town dogs—wow."

"And we have the most amazing dog trainer to staff it!" Gabby squeezed Hannah's shoulder. "I'm so excited for you!"

Reese held up a hand. "But there's a catch."

There were a couple of groans around the room. "There always is," Samantha said, sighing.

"We have to get the storage barn cleared out and the main work done by the end of the year," Reese said.

Gabby put a hand on her hip. "Why so fast?"

"That's when Aunt Catherine leaves for her winter home in Florida, and she wants it done before she goes. So we'll need all hands on deck to clear the barn, and Hannah, you'll need a pretty solid plan of what kind of facility you need."

Hannah had seen the storage barn, and she knew its structure was basically sound, though the place was filled with junk. Getting the project going so quickly would be a big challenge, but the fact that she'd helped renovate a facility on the outskirts of Cleveland a couple of years ago would be a big help. "I have no problem working day and night—" Hannah clapped a hand to her forehead and closed her eyes for a minute. "Well, except that I'm raising my nieces right now." For a few seconds, she'd forgotten that.

"There is that," Reese said, a smile tugging at his lips. "But on the other hand, if we can get this off the ground, there's a full-time job with benefits in it for you."

"Working right here by the twins' day care," Samantha added. "Oh, Hannah, that would be so, so perfect for you."

"It's just in the idea stage now," Reese warned, "so don't get too excited. They want to do it, but we haven't discussed details. Let's all head over and look at the old barn, see what would be involved, so we can make some kind of reasonable schedule if they decide to go forward."

"I'm out," Samantha said. "I need to get back to the kids."

So Reese, Gabby, Luke, Hannah and Dylan headed over, tromping through the icy brown grass. A cold wind whipped across the fields, and a lone crow landed on a stand of scraggly trees across the neighboring pasture.

Reese threw open the tall double doors of the storage barn and they all trooped in. It *was* a barn of sorts; its rough wooden walls were equipped with hooks to hold tack, and a wooden ladder led to a loft above. The faint smell of hay permeated the air, along with enough dust that Hannah's eyes watered.

But it bore no real resemblance to a working barn. Packed to the rafters with debris from long-ago owners who'd farmed the place, plus all kinds of rarely used items from the Rescue Haven program, it looked anything but promising for a dog-training facility.

"Luke, you're in charge," Reese said. "Gabby, you take notes. No physical work, promise me." He smiled tenderly at his wife.

Gabby opened her mouth like she was going to protest, but then her hands went to her pregnant belly and she nodded. "Okay, I guess."

Hannah felt a surprising flash of envy. Gabby seemed so settled now, so happy. Whereas Hannah felt anything but.

Especially since their field of workers was rapidly narrowing down. Luke, Reese, Gabby and Hannah walked around, surveying the mess. Dylan had made a phone call, but now he hurried in behind them. "I can help some while I'm here," he said. "Corbin's off-and-on busy at the university, so I'll have a little time if you need me."

Hannah didn't know what to wish for. Would it be more awkward to work with both Luke and Dylan, or just Luke? She was thankful for Reese and Gabby, who would buffer any weirdness between them all.

Hannah wasn't sure why it felt awkward. Probably because of that bizarre lead-in to her date with Dylan, in which Luke had loomed like a protective father and she'd had to practically shove him out the door.

Luke was still being mostly quiet—they all were—so when Reese's phone pinged it was audible to all of them. He looked at it. "Showtime," he said to the rest of them. "It's Aunt Catherine here to meet with me. I should be able to get more details on what they're looking for." He hurried out of the barn, talking into his phone.

"Looks like the main thing is going to be hauling stuff out of here," Luke said.

"And sorting," Gabby said. "We should get a dumpster for trash, but we'll be able to donate some of the equipment to local farmers. And some of the Rescue Haven stuff...well, Reese has been talking about building a shed that's just for our supplies. Maybe this is the time for that."

"That might be the first step," Luke said. "I can work on that. But, meanwhile, we can haul out some of the bigger stuff. Then we'll be able to see what we're dealing with."

"Maybe we could sell some things, even have an auction," Hannah suggested.

"Good idea." Luke gave her a brief smile that shot warmth all through her.

They worked together lifting an old dresser that might be an antique, underneath all the dust. Behind it, steel pilings lined one section of the floor. Hannah took a shot at lifting one and decided to leave the heavy items to the men.

Hannah walked over to some things Gabby was looking at. "Nana will have to decide about some of this," Gabby said. "Pretty sure she's never going to have a parrot again, not since we have Biff."

"True." Biff was their big, lovable dog who was forever chasing Nana's sour old cat, Mr. Pickles. "I'll carry out the cages, then," Hannah said.

Gabby tagged along. "It's so weird not being able to help," she fretted. "I feel kind of useless."

Hannah smiled over at her. "You're doing the most important work of all. You're growing a baby."

Gabby rolled her eyes. "I wasn't this coddled the first time, when I had Izzy, believe me."

Hannah knew Gabby had struggled, mostly alone, during her first pregnancy. "Enjoy Reese's protecting you. You deserve it."

"I guess. I think I'll make a list of what's here to show Nana." They walked back inside and Hannah picked up a second big birdcage and carried it out. Across the barn, Luke and Dylan were carrying an ancient-looking hay baler.

She slowed down, watching them. Two good men. She'd had a great time on her date with Dylan...once they'd both confessed that they were terminally awkward with the opposite sex, hated dates set up by someone else and probably weren't destined to be anything but friends.

She set down the second cage and headed inside for another load.

Why couldn't she have romantic feelings for Dylan? He was as muscular as Luke, which was obvious as they lifted and hauled. He was smart and kind.

Luke, on the other hand...well, he was muscular, smart and... *Was* he kind? Yes, as evidenced by the way he'd helped her during the kitten incident way back when. But there was an edge to him. Maybe it was just the fact that he'd been a popular bad boy in his teenage years.

Even if she'd been able to attract the interest of a popular guy like Luke, which was about as likely as winning a luxury cruise to the Canary Islands, she could never get into a relationship with him. Not given the secret she was hiding about the twins.

"Nice scenery, huh?" Gabby said.

Jolted out of her staring reverie, Hannah

felt her face heat. "Hey, you're married, you shouldn't be looking," she joked, kind of meaning it.

"Oh, neither one of them is even close to as handsome as my husband," Gabby said, smiling. "But there's nothing wrong with admiring strong, good-looking men."

Was that true? It was something Hannah had always stifled in herself. Maybe it was time to get past that outdated reaction if even happily married Gabby felt comfortable taking a look.

Gabby pulled out her phone. "Uh-oh. I almost forgot I need to go to the doctor with Nana," she said. "See you later. Don't forget to enjoy the view."

Hannah watched her go, still feeling uncomfortably warm. Would she ever be as content and relaxed as her friend?

"Hey, Hannah," Dylan called. "Can you give Luke a hand with this? I have a video meeting at ten and I need to do a little prep."

"Trying to get out of work, are you?" she teased as she walked over to him. Her heart was beating a little faster, and it *wasn't* because of Dylan.

"You know from Friday night, that's my tendency," he replied with a smile. Which was definitely a joke; he'd told Hannah about his own workaholism, which was something they had in common.

Luke stood waiting for her to take the other end of the wooden bench they were moving. He observed their interaction impassively, arms crossed. It was an awkward moment as they both watched Dylan exit the barn.

The doors creaked as he closed them. Great. Now it was just her and Luke.

Luke took his end of the bench and carried it out with Hannah holding the other end.

He tried to focus on the buckets and electrical cords and galvanized-steel cans of feed, but Hannah's flushed cheeks and sparkling eyes kept drawing his attention.

They set down the bench and walked back in together.

He should say something, to show he was a grown-up and not jealous of Dylan. "How was your *date*?" was what came out.

He was an idiot. He needed to overcome that primal urge to fight with another man over a potential mate. "Sorry, not my business," he said.

"No, it's okay." Hannah forked her fingers through her hair. "It was great, actually."

Of course, it had been great. Dylan was everything Luke wasn't. "You have a lot in common," he said, forcing himself to be agreeable.

"Yeah, we do." She knelt down beside an old tractor. "I wonder if this thing could be started up and driven out? Because it's going to be real hard to haul it."

He studied the tractor's compression-release valve. If she could be businesslike and professional, so could he. He wasn't going to look at those long eyelashes. Lots of women had long eyelashes.

Well, not as long as Hannah's, but long.

"We're both awkward as all get out with the opposite sex," Hannah said. "And too blunt. Me and Dylan," she clarified.

"Huh?" Luke wasn't sure what she was talking about. "What do you mean?"

"You wouldn't understand." She rocked back on her heels. "You were always so smooth with girls, to hear Marnie tell it. Whereas me... I get nervous and say the wrong thing."

"I wasn't smooth," he protested. "Or at least, not in a good way." He knew he'd hurt some girls' feelings in his early days of dating. He'd been way too full of himself.

"You had gazillions of girlfriends," she went on.

"I'm not proud of that." He climbed up into the seat of the tractor to look at the gearshift and clutch, both levers orange with rust. "I'm trying to be different now that I've...grown up." What he meant was, now that he'd come to Christ, but he wasn't quite comfortable saying that yet.

"Okay," she said, peering behind the tractor, "but you can turn on the charm if you want to get a date. I don't have it to turn on. And neither does Dylan."

Dylan. Luke repressed a snort. "Sounds like it worked just fine for you two without that."

"Sounds like what?" She came back out from behind the tractor just as he climbed off it. "Oh, no, we admitted right away that we aren't attracted to each other. I guess in that way, it's good we're both the blunt type."

Luke couldn't answer because of the relief that was rising up in him. Instead, he pulled out a rag and began polishing the old tractor, just for something to do.

"We could carry this out," she said, indicating a tall sideboard, so they did. Luke tried to keep from smiling, but it was impossible.

Dylan and Hannah weren't attracted to each other. They weren't going to get involved.

After setting down the sideboard, Luke and Hannah turned back toward the barn. "I just don't know how to do it," she said. "I don't know how to turn it on, to flirt. But I feel like I should, for the twins' sake."

"You mean if a man does this you don't know how to respond?" He moved a little closer as they walked side by side and put a hand on the small of her back.

She cringed and moved away.

He dropped his hand and took a giant step to the side, his face heating. "Sorry, sorry. I didn't mean to upset you. That's just something a man does, sometimes, kind of to try things out, see if there's interest." He shook his head. "I didn't mean to be creepy. I'm sorry."

He was a jerk. And he was even more of a jerk because he'd liked the way it felt to touch her spine, to feel the ridge of muscles on either side of it, at least during the nanosecond before her horrified reaction.

"No, it's me." She waved a hand, her face flushing pink. "See, I don't get it. I don't know how to act if a guy does something like that, something totally innocent."

Something about her tone gave Luke a bad feeling. "Did something happen?"

She opened her mouth to answer, but a shout from Reese stopped their conversation.

He wondered what she'd been going to say. What had made Hannah wary, so that she tensed up around men?

Reese looked around the barn. "So it's down to you two, is it? I hope you're both okay with spending a lot of time together."

Luke gulped. He was very okay and not okay at all with it.

"What do you mean?" Hannah asked, her voice uneasy.

"Mr. Romano and Aunt Catherine are throwing out their usual challenge."

"A trial with a deadline?" Hannah asked.

"Uh-huh. And there's another side to it, too. They got an estimate of what a facility like that would cost from a couple of different sources, and they want us to build one on half of that. Bricks without straw."

Luke surprised himself by catching the bible reference. "Why are they playing Pharaoh?"

Reese ran his hands through his hair. "They think this will help make Rescue Haven self-sustaining. I tried to argue, but then they started talking about how they were going to die, and they wanted the programs they started to live on."

Two lines etched between Hannah's eyebrows. "Wow."

"I didn't know what to say. Except, okay, sure, we can do that."

"What's the deadline?" Luke asked.

Reese looked from Luke to Hannah and back again. "Month and a half. They want a state-of-the-art facility for dog training by the end of the year," he said. "And from the looks of things, from our staffing and all our other projects, the work is going to fall on the two of you."

Hannah sucked in a breath, her face going pale.

"Big job." Luke looked back at the barn. "Though once it's cleared out, the bones are solid, and that'll help. Right?" He looked at Hannah.

"Yes. But we'll need new flooring, and some of the walls will have to be repaired. Plus, we'll need to install all the equipment."

"The good news for both of you," Reese said, "is that if we can accomplish what they want, there will be two permanent job openings, full-time, with benefits. One for a dog trainer, and one for a property manager."

"I'll do it," Hannah said immediately. "I have to. It's a way to support the twins."

"Luke?" Reese asked.

He blew out a breath. "I… Sure, I'll work on it," he said. "No need to get ahead of ourselves about the permanent-job thing, though."

Because if working closely with Hannah for a month and a half was going to be hard, working with her permanently would be even harder.

Chapter Five

Tuesday evening after dinner, Hannah opened the door to Luke and felt a flutter in her chest.

He was such a *man* compared to guys her age, with his heavy beard stubble, the slight creases at the corners of his eyes and the confidence of his smile.

Oh, he was a charmer, she thought as he held her gaze a little too long. Or was it she who'd looked too long at him?

"Come on in," she said, and turned so he wouldn't see her flushed face. "We can work in the kitchen, but I'm warning you, things are a little chaotic." Working in the same room with Mom, Addie and Emmy wasn't ideal, but it was a way they could get started. Mom had agreed to put the twins to bed after she got a few things done, so that Luke and Hannah could work together.

If they wanted to accomplish their goal of planning and renovating the new dog-training facility by the end of the year, they couldn't wait until after Thanksgiving; they had to get started right away.

In the kitchen, Mom was helping Emmy stack blocks while Addie looked on with that telltale grin that said she wanted to knock them down. When Luke came in, Mom stood and gave him a spontaneous hug. "It's good to see you, honey," she said, friendly and unselfconscious with him in a way that Hannah envied. "I'm glad you could be here for your dad. How's he doing?"

Luke shrugged and gave a lopsided grin. "About what you'd expect. He's scared, and he hates being restricted on what he can do, so he's not in the best mood. But we're hoping the surgery will solve his problems and that everything's benign."

"When is his surgery?" Mom asked.

"Right after the holiday weekend. Monday, sometime in the morning. The hospital will call with the schedule the day before."

"I'll keep him in my prayers," Mom said. "And you, too. Being a caregiver isn't easy."

"That's for sure," Luke said with a sigh that said he meant it.

Addie pushed herself to her feet and toddled over to Hannah, holding up her arms. Hannah swung her up. "You're such a big girl!" she said, kissing Addie's cheek and then settling her on her hip.

Emmy watched, and her face scrunched a little.

"Oh, honey, you need some attention, too, don't you?" Mom hurried over and knelt beside her. "I'd pick you up, but my back hurts." She pulled Emmy into her lap and cuddled her close.

"What are you cooking?" Luke stepped toward the stove and turned down the gas burner. "It's boiling pretty hard."

"Oh, my word." Mom shifted Emmy back to the floor, stood and hurried to the stove. "Thank you. It's a white sauce for mac and cheese. And I've got cranberries cooking and a pie in the oven."

"Smells great," Luke said, smiling.

Hannah opened her mouth to ask Luke and his father to Thanksgiving dinner and then closed it again. She and Mom always invited people who didn't have a place to go or didn't like to cook, but with Luke, she hesitated.

Emmy got to her feet and toddled toward them.

"Your turn?" Hannah shifted Addie on her hip. Holding both girls at once was a challenge, but she'd try.

Emmy had other ideas. She reached up both hands to Luke.

His face lit up. "Come to Uncle Luke," he said as he leaned down and lifted her into his arms.

Hannah froze. Did he know something?

But he was tickling Emmy under her chin, making her giggle. Watching them together crashed a new problem into Hannah's consciousness. Something she should have thought of, but hadn't had the bandwidth.

What would happen when the twins were older, old enough to ask about their daddy? Was it right to keep them from the only parent they had left, and to keep the truth about him a secret, as well?

And even if it was—because Bobby wasn't ever going to be father of the year—what about their uncle? Now that she'd gotten closer to Luke, she realized that for the twins, not knowing their connection to him would be a loss.

Mom pulled the pie out of the oven and then turned their way. A smile creased her flushed face. "See, they need a man in their lives."

Luke glanced over at her. "Hannah said their father isn't involved. Is that permanent?"

Hannah held her breath. When she'd suggested they meet here, she'd had no idea of how difficult and awkward it would be.

Mom shook her head. "Marnie would never

talk about him. I've speculated and thought back on what little I know about her life in Indianapolis…" Her voice went high and tight and she turned away, her eyes shiny.

"I'm sorry to bring up a painful subject." Luke patted her awkwardly on the back.

Hannah set down Addie and pulled out her favorite toy, a big plastic bowl and a wooden spoon. She put the bowl upside down and handed the spoon to Addie, who immediately started beating on the bowl. Emmy struggled in Luke's arms, and he set her down beside her twin. Quickly, Hannah handed her a set of measuring spoons on a ring and some nested measuring cups, and she started jingling the spoons, holding them close to her ear.

"It's noisy," Hannah said to Luke, above the din, "but it's the best way to keep them happy while we work." She gestured to a seat at the table, then pulled out her own chair kitty-corner from him. She turned on her laptop. "How's Goldie's training coming along?"

He shook his head. "We're not making a whole lot of progress."

"Maybe another training session tomorrow, since we don't have work?" Hannah really liked the sweet pit bull and wanted to see her training succeed.

"That would be great. She needs it." He smiled

at her. "Guess we should get started on our plans for the facility."

"Yes." Hannah turned the screen so he could see it. "I'm going to set up a shared file so we can both add to it. Links, or receipts, or whatever."

"Great."

They made a list of steps and agreed they needed to visit at least one other training facility to get ideas. But just as they hit their stride, brainstorming ideas, the twins started pulling at them, babbling in a whiny way.

After her third attempt to suggest a plan of action, Hannah sighed and picked up Emmy. "This may have been a bad idea," she said. "Maybe we should work at your place from here on out."

Luke shook his head. "That might be worse," he said. "Granted, we should do most of our work during the days, at Rescue Haven. But I can't be mad at these little ones." He grabbed a dishtowel and put it over his hand, like a puppet. "Right?" he said in a puppet voice to Addie. "It's not your fault you're babies!" He used the towel to tickle her hand.

She howled with laughter. "More!"

"I'll take over in ten minutes," Mom promised. "If I could just run upstairs and get their bath ready…"

"Go. That's fine." Luke waved her away. "Isn't it?" he asked Hannah.

"If it's okay with you," she said. The truth was, it was kind of fun to have Luke here helping to entertain the twins. Most evenings, they got fretful at this time, and she and Mom scrambled to manage baths and evening routines.

If there was a man around to help raise them... yeah. She could definitely see the appeal.

But she was never going to have that. She was terminally awkward and had never had a successful date in her life. And she wasn't going to pity herself for that. "How come you're so good with babies?" she asked Luke, to change the subject.

He looked down at the table and rubbed the heel of his palm against his chest. "Oh, I've dated a few women with kids. Before...well, before I got a better idea about how things should be."

"None of your own?" As soon as she said it, she clapped a hand over her mouth, causing Emmy to try to do the same. "Sorry. That was way too personal of a question."

"It's okay." He shrugged. "I knew I wasn't in a place to make a baby, in all kinds of ways. Babies need both parents." He looked at the twins. "In an ideal world, that is."

Addie got fussy then, and Luke carried her over to the sliding glass doors to look out, bouncing her a little. Emmy pointed. She wanted to go, too.

So Hannah carried her over as she struggled with her own conflicted feelings.

She'd made a promise to Marnie, and she took that seriously. Marnie wasn't here to release her from it.

At the same time, she could see how great Luke would be as an uncle to these little girls. They needed all the adult support they could get.

It was an impossible situation.

"Hey," he said, close to her ear. They were standing shoulder-to-shoulder, each with a twin. "I'm sorry I said that about both parents. The world *isn't* ideal. You're doing the best you can."

"Thanks." Their eyes met, held. She could smell his aftershave, something woodsy, mixing with the good scents from Mom's cooking. She could see the deep mahogany-brown of his eyes. They were thoughtful eyes, more than she would have expected. Just like she wouldn't have expected him to be so good with babies. Luke had a lot of layers.

His eyes flickered down to her lips, and she felt a happy shiver. Quickly, though, it was replaced by a tight, sick feeling.

She couldn't go there. Not with Luke, not with anyone.

"Look, Addie's flushed. She's so tired." Hannah sucked in a breath and stepped away. Her heart was racing. "Uh, I better take them upstairs. Do you mind if we put off the rest of our planning until tomorrow?"

"No problem." His eyes narrowed a little.

If she hadn't known better, she'd have thought he looked hurt. Was it because she'd backed away?

Unfortunately, he had looked like he knew she was attracted, too, which made sense. Luke was experienced.

Working closely together was going to be very, very dangerous.

The next day, Luke watched Hannah as she discussed the dog-training site they were visiting with one of the trainers who worked there. She was animated, waving her arms and smiling, a woman in love with her work.

Different from how she'd looked last night. Then, there'd been a flash of interest, maybe even attraction.

Or maybe he'd imagined it.

He was actually surprised she'd wanted to get together with him today, after the way she'd skittered off last night. It had bothered him as he'd let himself out and walked through the trees to his father's place.

When he'd gone inside, seen the piles of dirty

dishes and empty beer cans that meant Dad had gone on another bender, he'd felt like his own identity was a weight on his shoulders. When he contrasted their kitchen to Hannah's, when he contrasted his family to hers…well, no wonder she'd backed away from him like he carried a deadly disease.

But she'd sent a friendly text, apologizing for bailing out of their work session and not seeing him out, and suggested that they meet today to look at a dog-training facility. They planned to swing by a big-box store on the way home to price supplies, and if they had the energy, to squeeze in a lesson for Goldie afterward.

A dog jumped over bars and through tunnels on the other side of the ring, a woman running along beside, shouting encouragement. The space was huge, clean and airy, and not at all what they'd be able to build in the old barn. Still, Hannah had been right to insist that they come here and look around, just to get an idea of what they were going for.

Hannah was driven, businesslike and efficient. Combine all of those qualities with pretty and smart, and she was a great package. He couldn't really fathom why she wasn't married or at least dating someone.

Then again, she'd talked about an issue she had with dating, something from her past. If some guy had hurt Hannah—sweet, innocent Hannah—Luke would like to have a word with him. A strong word.

"Luke? What do you think?" Hannah was looking at him, her head tilted to one side, a pair of lines between her eyebrows. It might not be the first time she'd asked the question.

"Sorry, daydreaming," he said, and refocused on the floor covering and the subfloor, the way the place was ventilated so it didn't hold doggy odors. They walked across the artificial grass to where the woman and dog had been running around, and the trainer explained that the equipment was for a dog sport called agility.

That there *were* even dog sports was news to Luke, but he studied the structures, a double-sided ramp and a bar that could be moved to different heights, a sort of teeter-totter, and the rubbery tunnels for dogs to run through.

"It's all pretty expensive if you order it on-line," the trainer said, "but I can hook you up with a local distributor who has some used stuff."

"I could build it." Luke studied the underside of the ramp, scooted out and walked over to the teeter-totter. "None of this is complicated, and we probably have half the materials already in the barn. There's a lot of lumber there."

"That would be perfect, especially since we're

on such a tight budget!" Hannah smiled and clapped her hands a little. "Thank you!"

"I'm jealous," the trainer said. "I wish I had a good handyman." She studied Luke with frank admiration, but it was a different type of admiration than what Hannah was exhibiting. The trainer, Celia, was closer to Luke's age, curvy and cute. She was his type, or at least, his old type.

"Let me give you my number in case you have any questions," she said, scribbling on a business card and handing it, not to Hannah, but to Luke.

Hannah raised an eyebrow but didn't say anything.

"In fact," Celia said, pushing it, "do you ever go to Rodney's Grille? It's a country-western place just off 80. If you'd want to meet me there sometime…" She trailed off and gave him a look of frank, womanly challenge.

There had been a time, not that long ago, when Luke would have taken her up on her offer. She looked like she liked to have fun, and he'd never minded a woman being a little forward.

Now, though… He glanced at Hannah and stepped a little closer to her. "That's a nice offer," he said, "but we're going to be pretty busy working on the new site."

Celia's eyes flickered from Luke to Hannah and back again. "Oooh, well, okay," she said.

Her voice sounded skeptical. "If you change your mind, you have my number."

"Thanks."

"Thanks for your help," Hannah added.

Out in the car, she smacked him on the arm. "She was hitting on you and you put her down!"

"Maybe," he said. "Best not to get started if you don't intend to go forward." And as he drove them back toward Bethlehem Springs, he tried to keep that sage bit of advice in his mind.

He'd do well to apply that to his current situation, not only with the other dog trainer, but also with Hannah. The temptation to ask her out, maybe even to Rodney's Grille for some country dancing, was strong in him. But it would never work long-term, because he was a Hutchenson. Best, then, not to start at all.

Chapter Six

On Thanksgiving morning, Hannah kept herself as busy as she could, which wasn't hard. She bundled up the twins and took them outside to run off some energy in the icy air. Emmy got fascinated with the frost on the grass, crawling around to examine it. Addie climbed the little plastic play structure's ladder and slid down the slide, over and over again.

Once they seemed sufficiently tired, Hannah took them inside and sat them in a corner of the kitchen, where Emmy stacked plastic blocks and Addie played with a baby doll. That gave Hannah the opportunity to peel potatoes and chop celery, helping Mom prepare for the midafternoon Thanksgiving dinner.

Staying busy helped her forget things she didn't want to think about, like Luke Hutchenson. They'd had such a good time yesterday, laughing together and planning and driving all over after the training-facility visit, hunting down the supplies they'd need to get started. Luke was fun—take-charge when he needed to be, easygoing the rest of the time. She'd forgotten her usual nerves around attractive men and relaxed into the companionship, and it had thawed something inside her she hadn't known was frozen.

She hadn't thawed quite enough to invite Luke and his dad to dinner, though, and it was bothering her.

Even more than Luke, she was thinking about her sister. Although Marnie hadn't come home for Thanksgiving since she'd moved to Indianapolis, before that, she'd almost always showed up for Thanksgiving dinner with a store-bought relish tray or a bag of ingredients for green-bean casserole, apologizing for the fact that she hadn't come earlier to help, and joking around until everyone forgave her.

Thanksgiving wasn't the same without her. More organized, maybe, but less fun, less colorful, less spontaneous.

Hannah checked on the twins, giving them extra kisses on the tops of their curly blond heads. It didn't do much good to grieve over their mother when the current goal was to take good care of these little ones. Marnie should have prioritized that herself, but she hadn't. So Hannah pressed her lips together and tried to focus on the smell of onions and celery sautéed in butter, and the turkey just starting to send its fabulous aroma through the house.

Half an hour later, car doors slammed outside, and then the back door opened. "We're here!" Samantha called out, unnecessarily. You couldn't have missed their arrival, given she'd brought not only Corbin, but also Mikey and their dog, Boomer.

Addie and Emmy got very excited, although also a little scared, when the big black dog came over and sniffed at them.

Mikey, full of his important role as the older cousin, explained that Boomer wasn't dangerous, but that they should touch him gently under the chin and shouldn't pull on his abundant black coat.

Boomer flopped down beside the girls, to their shrieking delight.

"Girls," Mom said, "you're going to scare the dog! Quiet down."

"It's not a problem," Samantha said. "He's deaf, remember? Now, where can I put the green-bean casserole?"

"You brought Marnie's dish!" Hannah teared up as she took the casserole and set it in the refrigerator.

"Yeah." Samantha folded Mom into a hug, both of them shiny-eyed.

Hannah took everyone's coats, and then she and Samantha discussed Rescue Haven as they set the table.

"Getting the training center will be a good opportunity for you, right?" Samantha asked.

"Huge." Hannah carefully lined up Mom's harvest-themed napkins, the same ones they'd used every Thanksgiving for as long as she could remember. "Right now, I'm my own business, which means I have to pay for my own insurance, do my own billing, everything. Having a full-time job with benefits would let me focus on what I love—training dogs. And I could be more available for the twins."

"We just have to make it happen, then." Samantha gave a decisive nod. "Anything I can do to help, let me know."

"Believe me, being able to put Addie and Emmy into the Learn-and-Play, knowing you're there looking after them… I'm incredibly grateful."

"Don't forget to fill the salt-and-pepper shakers," Mom called. So Hannah looked through Mom's collection until she found the turkey ones. They went into the kitchen to fill them.

All of a sudden, Samantha clapped her hand

to her forehead. "Oh, I wonder what Luke and his father are doing for Thanksgiving?"

"I didn't even think of that," Mom said. "My hospitality has gone right out of my head with… everything. It's probably too late to invite them, isn't it?"

Looking from Mom's worried face to Samantha's, Hannah felt a stab of guilt. She'd thought of inviting Luke, had had the opportunity both yesterday and the day before, but she hadn't done it.

For good reason. They can't know the truth about the twins.

But having them here for the holiday wouldn't make them any more likely to find out, would it?

Mom opened the oven to slide in a dish of sweet potatoes, and the wonderful aroma of roasted turkey wafted out. Someone turned on a country music station, and it played low beneath the buzz of conversation and laughter.

Meanwhile, Luke was next door, alone, with his ill, difficult father.

It wasn't right. She had to fix it. "I'll invite them," Hannah said, grabbing her coat from the hook by the door.

Five minutes later, she knocked timidly on the door of Luke's place.

Goldie started barking, and then Luke's father answered. He was wearing an undershirt and ragged pants, and he was barefoot. And he didn't look friendly. "What?" he asked through the screen door.

"Hi, um, happy Thanksgiving!" A blast of cold wind swept her hair across her face, and she pushed it back behind her ear, shivering.

He just looked at her. Goldie let out another bark and then settled into tail-wagging.

"Um, Mom and I were wondering if you and Luke might want to come over for dinner. We've got a huge turkey, and we'd love to have some help eating it."

Luke's father blew out a puff of air and looked off to the side.

"If you don't want to or you have other plans, it's fine. You probably do have other plans." She was babbling.

Luke came around the side of the house. He was wearing a flannel shirt and jeans, and even in the cold air, it looked like he was sweating. Hannah's throat went dry. He'd been attractive playing with the babies the other day, but now...

"Hey, Hannah," he said. "Sorry, I was chopping wood and didn't hear you. What's up?"

Hannah felt too breathless to speak. Luke as lumberjack claimed all of her mental energy.

"We got us an invite to a turkey dinner," Luke's father said.

Hannah pulled her eyes away from him and nodded. "We'd love to have you come. Dinner's at three, but you could come anytime. Only thing is, Goldie would have to stay home, because we've got another big dog over there today."

Luke looked at his father. "Want to go?"

The older man shrugged. "Beats the leftover pizza we've got in the refrigerator."

"Sure does." Luke looked at Hannah, tilting his head a little. "If you're sure, we'll get cleaned up and see you soon."

"Great!" Was it, though? She gave an awkward little wave and scurried away.

Dinner was like something out of a feel-good movie, and Luke loved it.

Hannah and her mom had put together a couple of tables to make one long one, and November sunshine came in through tall, old-fashioned windows. Hannah and Samantha put the twins into side-by-side high chairs with helpful suggestions from Samantha's son, Mikey. Once she got Emmy settled, Hannah ruffled Mikey's hair, laughing, and Luke's heart warmed.

"Come carry this turkey, Luke, Corbin, would you?" Hannah's mom called. "And then you can carve." The two of them hurried into the steamy kitchen and brought the giant, fragrant, golden-brown turkey to the table. Luke had carved a few birds in his day, but Corbin's scientific approach was decidedly superior. So Luke dropped back and made faces at Addie and Emmy, trying to keep them entertained until everyone could get to the table.

Dad, dressed in a clean, ironed shirt and some dress slacks Luke hadn't known he owned, had disappeared into the kitchen a few minutes ago, and Luke was half-waiting for him to do or say something inappropriate. But here he came behind Hannah's mom, carefully carrying a full-to-the-brim gravy boat, which he set on the table without spilling a drop.

The whole group held hands and prayed—even Dad—and everyone passed around dishes of food: roasted turkey, potatoes, rolls, cranberry sauce and stuffing and gravy.

Conversation flowed, and the food was the best he'd had in ages. Dad ate heartily, and seeing his appetite, Luke resolved to do better with preparing some healthy meals. Pizza didn't really cut it for a sick man.

As the dishes were passed around for a second time, everyone went into the usual Thanksgiving mode, groaning about how overstuffed they were. Mikey tried to wipe the twins' messy faces and ended up smearing cranberry sauce into Emmy's blond hair.

"I know I'm supposed to be eating for two," Samantha said, "but I think I ate for six. I'm gonna regret this."

"You and me both." Corbin leaned back and rested his hands on his stomach.

"I practically have a baby bump myself," Hannah joked, standing to clear away plates.

It wasn't true; she was tiny and slim-waisted in a red sweater and jeans.

Emmy fisted up green beans and stuffed them into her mouth. Addie, apparently finished eating, started dropping turkey to the floor, much to Boomer's delight.

After the table was cleared, Hannah and her mom brought in plates of pie and a big pot of coffee.

Dad cleared his throat. "Brought a little something for the grown-ups," he said. He pulled a flask from his pocket.

Conversation paused and Luke's stomach plunged as he tried to think of how to handle this. Taking the flask away would result in an ugly scene, he knew.

Hannah's mother held out her hand for the flask, and Dad relinquished it with a grin. "You can drink right from there or get you a glass, classy-like," he said.

But Hannah's mom kept the flask closed. "I know a lot of people like a drink," she said, looking around the table, "but in this house, we don't allow alcohol."

Dad's face got red and his eyebrows pushed together.

Luke tensed, ready to intervene. This was why they didn't get invited places; they weren't fit for company.

Samantha looked distressed, and Hannah seemed frozen. Only the twins babbled on, oblivious to the tension.

Hannah's mom reached out a hand to brush back Emmy's hair, then Addie's. "I lost my daughter, these precious girls' mother, to drugs and alcohol," she said, her voice quiet. Then she looked around the table again. "I lost her long before she actually passed, because she wanted this—" she held up the flask "—more than she wanted to be with us."

Hannah looked like she was about to cry.

"It's an illness," Samantha said quietly. "I know, because I overcame it." She reached over and squeezed Hannah's mother's hand.

Dad's grimace softened.

"You're right," Hannah's mom said. "For her it definitely was an illness." Then she leaned forward and addressed Luke's father. "I don't know if you have that illness or not. It's not my business. But I'm just going to ask you to put this back in your pocket to take home, and I apologize if that makes the day less festive for you."

The table was quiet. Luke barely breathed. *Don't make a scene*, he silently begged his father. *Don't hurt this family more.*

"But there *is* pie," Corbin said, breaking the tension, "and that's pretty festive."

"Pie!" Addie cried out.

"Pie!" Emmy echoed. She banged her hands on her high-chair tray.

Everyone laughed and just like that, they were back to a happy holiday meal. Hannah and Corbin cut the pies, one coconut cream and one pumpkin. Dad, now out of the spotlight and probably relieved he hadn't been made to feel like the bad guy, patted Hannah's mother's hand. "I understand what it is to lose a child," he said. "You know about my younger boy. Him being in prison isn't as bad as what you've faced, but it still gets you."

"Of course it does." Hannah's mom smiled at him, her eyes wet with tears that looked ready to spill over.

Luke couldn't believe it: Dad had cooled down and was getting along fine with Hannah's mom. A fight had been averted.

As he dug in to a big slice of coconut-cream pie, then snagged a piece of pumpkin with real whipped cream, Luke felt an unexpected blast of optimism. Could it be that all things would work here, that him staying and helping Dad get involved with better people would be best? And maybe he could even give it a go with Hannah…

He looked at her, laughing, kneeling beside Emmy while Addie looked on and clapped. Noise and happy chatter surrounded them.

It was like something out of a movie, and he felt a pang.

Even though they'd made it through one holiday meal without causing a disaster, people like his dad and him could never fit into a family like this.

Chapter Seven

The day after Thanksgiving, Hannah pulled into the last parking space on Main Street. Black Friday wasn't such a big deal in a small town as it would be in a city, but people did like to get out, shop, eat and share stories of their holiday dinners and dramas.

Hannah was hoping to distract herself from thinking about yesterday's dinner, which had mingled her family with the Hutchensons. While there'd been an awkward moment over the flask Luke's dad had brought, things had otherwise gone well.

And *that* was what she didn't want to think about. The family gathering had actually been biologically linked by the twins. If things had been different, if Hannah hadn't been keeping her sister's secret, Luke would know he was the girls' uncle and Luke's father, their grandfather.

Keeping that truth from the Hutchensons, as well as from Addie and Emmy, was seeming like more and more of a mistake.

"Over here!" Gabby called. She was standing with Sheniqua, a doctor in town and one of their friends, in front of Bethlehem Springs's small department store. Both women waved and beckoned. Hannah slid out of her car, automatically checked for her diaper bag and realized she didn't need it, because Mom was at home with the twins this morning.

She laughed at herself. She was becoming more of a mother every day. Feeling free, she wove through the other pedestrians toward her friends.

The street bustled with shoppers on this chilly November day. People greeted each other, some wearing red scarves or hats, others going full out with reindeer-antler headbands. Candy-cane decorations transformed the lampposts, and most of the storefronts and cafés sported Christmas displays.

Hannah's spirits lifted as she approached Sheniqua and Gabby, and they shared hugs all around. She wasn't going to think about Luke anymore. She was going to enjoy this time with her friends.

"That's it for Thanksgiving—it's time for Christmas," Sheniqua said as they walked into the crowded, noisy department store. "Did you all have a good holiday?"

"Ate too much, but yes." Gabby nudged Hannah. "I heard *you* had some last-minute visitors who livened things up."

Sheniqua raised an eyebrow. "Who would that be?"

"Luke Hutchenson and his dad came over," Hannah said as they turned, by unspoken agreement, toward the children's section.

"Ah, handsome Luke," Sheniqua said, raising and lowering her eyebrows in an exaggerated way.

Hannah looked at her sharply, then looked away.

"Hey, don't worry," Sheniqua said, patting her lightly on the arm. "I've got enough relationship problems. I'm not remotely interested in Luke."

"I didn't mean—" Hannah cut off her comment, flustered.

"Relationship problems?" Gabby looked over at Sheniqua, smiling and tilting her head to one side. "Do tell."

"Nope, nothing I want to talk about," Sheniqua said firmly.

"And I have nothing to talk about, either," Hannah said. It was true. Yes, Luke had come over, and yes, she was working closely with him. And, yes, there was a spark between them, at least on Hannah's side. But there was also a secret separating them.

Which meant it wasn't going to come to anything. It couldn't, even if "handsome Luke," as Sheniqua had called him, was interested.

Fortunately, Gabby started talking to a salesperson about the infant clothes. Hannah turned toward the toddler outfits, hoping to find something on sale for the twins. Sheniqua headed toward the men's department…intriguing, that. Who was she shopping for?

Hannah fingered some cute Christmas pajamas that said, Dear Santa, My Sister Did It with an arrow pointing to the side. They'd be perfect for the twins. Luke's dad would love them. He'd gotten a huge kick out of the turkey T-shirts the twins had been wearing yesterday.

She carried two pajama sets, one red and one green, to the counter, smiling to think of the reaction they'd evoke. It was only after she'd put away her wallet and the clerk was bagging the pajamas that she realized: of course, Luke and his father wouldn't be there to see them. Spending Thanksgiving together had been a fluke. They weren't going to start spending every holiday together.

That was how it had to be.

After shopping a little more, they went to Cleo's Crafts and Café for hot chocolate. Samantha was there, drinking a hot chocolate while Corbin and Mikey shopped, and Gabby gratefully sat down at the table with her. The two of them immediately started groaning over their advanced pregnancies and swollen ankles and heartburn.

Hannah sighed as she and Sheniqua went to the counter to pick up the drinks. "I'm happy for them," she said, "but I'm jealous, I'll admit it." She'd imagined countless times what it would be like to be pregnant, to give birth to a beautiful baby to care for and love.

"They're fortunate," Sheniqua said quietly. "Healthy pregnancies and supportive husbands."

That was the key. If she was going to have a baby, she needed a husband. And she was so pathetically awkward with men that she couldn't see that happening.

Besides, she had plenty of family to worry about now, without adding a baby into the mix. She needed to focus on Addie and Emmy. "I worry about the twins not having a male influence."

They could, if you'd tell the truth.

"You'll get there," Sheniqua said with confidence. "You already have two beautiful babies. The right man will come along."

They carried the drinks back toward their table.

"I don't know a man who'd want to take on twin toddlers," Hannah said as they took their seats.

Gabby and Samantha had been talking, but at Hannah's words, they both turned toward her. "*Luke* seems to like the girls," Samantha said, grinning wickedly.

"Do tell." Sheniqua sipped her salted caramel latte and leaned forward.

"Well, not only did he help with the twins," Hannah's traitorous cousin said, "but you should have seen how he looked at Hannah."

Hannah's cheeks heated as she waved her hand back and forth. "He didn't look at me any particular way," she said, even as she wondered: *did* he? How had he looked at her?

"Oh, he sure did." Samantha launched into an exaggerated story of how Luke had jumped up to help with the dishes the moment Hannah had, how he'd looked at Hannah like she was a piece of coconut-cream pie. Samantha was being silly. Wasn't she? Nothing in particular had happened. Although maybe Samantha had really seen something in Luke's behavior that made her think he liked Hannah.

Gabby checked the time on her phone and stood. "I'm going to have to take this to go," she said. "Izzy's having a friend over, and I don't want to leave Nana to handle two toddlers on her own." She put on her coat, grabbed her hot chocolate and leaned down. "By the way," she said to Hannah, but loud enough for the others to hear, "a *person of interest* just came in." She spun and headed out.

Oh, no. Hannah knew exactly whom Gabby was talking about.

She looked toward the door and watched Gabby greet Luke and gesture toward their table, and her face heated.

Sheniqua and Samantha looked from Luke to Hannah, and then at each other.

"You know," Sheniqua said, "I think I'll take my drink to go, too."

"I feel a sudden urge to leave, as well," Samantha said.

"Wait! Don't go!" Hannah grabbed Samantha's hand and reached for Sheniqua's. With extraordinary effort, she avoided looking at Luke.

"Far be it from us to interfere with the course of true love," Sheniqua said, stepping out of Hannah's reach.

"Later." Samantha pulled her hand away, laughing, and the two of them hurried off, leaving Hannah at the table alone.

She wasn't going to look at Luke. She wasn't going to acknowledge that he was here, not unless he came over to the table. Which she *didn't* want him to do.

Then she *did* glance at him, and found him

looking across the shop at her. He gave her a little wave and that crooked smile that did something to her insides. The smile that suggested something was happening in *his* insides, too.

He held up a finger, as if to tell her to wait, he was coming over.

Her face warmed and she gave a little nod, hoping he couldn't see her blush from across the room.

When he didn't approach after several minutes, she stole a glance at the counter. There he stood, talking to the worker there, a pretty blonde woman who was being far more animated than she'd been when Hannah and Sheniqua had gone up for their drinks.

Luke was smiling and nodding. The two of them were the same age, probably high-school friends. If not more.

The blonde flirted easily, flipping her hair, looking away and then back, smiling a secret little smile. *She* didn't have issues in her past that made her awkward around men.

She was way more sophisticated than Hannah would ever be.

Good, she thought. *Talk to her, not me.* Hannah grabbed her drink and coat, and hurried toward the door of the shop.

"Hey, Hannah!" It was Luke calling behind her. But she didn't look back.

Maybe Luke had a little bit of interest in her, at least when no other women were around. Maybe it was a novelty to someone like him to have an awkward younger woman crushing on him.

But it wasn't anything real. It couldn't be.

She needed to make sure to remember that.

Monday, waiting for his dad to recover from surgery, Luke had plenty of time to think.

Dad had blustered and complained all the way to the hospital and had annoyed most of the staff he'd come into contact with. Yet, looking past the superficial angry attitude, Luke had seen real fear in his father's eyes, and understandably so. There were serious risks associated with having part of your liver surgically removed, and a long recovery period, especially for someone whose overall health wasn't the greatest.

Dad had mentioned Luke's brother several times, and Luke had finally realized his father needed to visit him. He'd made that promise to Dad, and it had tamed some of the angst in the man's eyes.

A text from Reese at Rescue Haven, wishing his dad well and asking if there was anything Luke needed, reminded Luke that he was working for good people. He denied needing anything, but despite that, Reese stopped by midafternoon with a big sandwich Gabby had made, and a jug of homemade lemonade.

"Thanks, man. I hate hospital cafeteria food." Luke took a few big bites of the sandwich and then looked at Reese. "I'll get all my hours in, just on a different schedule," he promised. "Pretty sure there's a visiting nurse who will give me a break."

"We'll manage, man. I'm not here to criticize." Reese sat down across from Luke and looked around the sterile, fluorescent-lit waiting room. "Just thought you might want a little company. Waiting stinks."

"It does. Thanks for that." But just because Reese was kind didn't mean Luke was going to shirk his responsibilities. "I know the project with Hannah has a tight deadline."

"It does. That's the thing to focus on, for sure, if you can."

They talked for a few more minutes and then, after Reese left, Luke thought about Hannah. He'd seen her at Cleo's on Friday, but she'd left quickly, before he could talk to her.

Had that been on purpose? If so, why? They'd gotten along just fine at the Thanksgiving dinner. In fact, it had been a highlight of Luke's time in Bethlehem Springs, and had been good for Dad, too.

The surgeon came out, smiling, and Luke

breathed a sigh of relief. He hadn't known how anxious he felt about his father even surviving the surgery until this moment. "Everything went well," the surgeon said, and launched into some medical details Luke could barely take in.

"Can I see him?" he asked when the man came to a good stopping point.

"He'll be in recovery for several hours," the surgeon said. "Once we get him to a room, you can visit, although he'll be groggy. And I don't want to minimize the seriousness of the surgery. It went well, but with your dad's health issues, we want to keep him here for several days, at least."

Luke shot up a prayer of thanks after the man left. Then he sent Hannah a text. Dad's surgery went well. Stuck here. Anything I can work on?

Give me ten minutes, she texted back.

Ten minutes later, she walked through the waiting-room door. "Sorry to assume, but Reese said you were okay with visitors." She placed a container of cookies and a large-print devotional book on the table beside him. "These are from Mom's bakery. I take no credit, but they're delicious."

"Thanks." He moved the book, opened the container and nodded appreciatively. "Sugar cookies. Simple and good. Have one."

She did, and they crunched in silence for a

minute. Then she set hers down. "The book's for your dad," she said, and held up her hand. "I know, he's not a churchgoer. But sometimes, when you're bored and scared, a little support from Scripture can help."

"Battlefield conversion?"

"Something like that." She smiled. "Who knows, maybe you'll be bored and want to read it, too."

"Right." He didn't feel like talking about faith with Hannah, even though he was truly grateful to God for bringing Dad through the surgery okay. "I saw you at Cleo's Friday, but you left before I could say hello."

She shrugged, her face reddening. "You seemed busy."

"I did?" He cast his mind back. He'd just stopped in, truth to tell, to put off going home to his grouchy father. To assuage his guilt about that, he'd gotten Dad one of Cleo's good coffees.

"That woman behind the counter," she said.

He thought again. "Oh, Bridget." He nodded. "We went to high school together. Way before you were anything but a kid." He was teasing her about how young she was, but she didn't seem to like it, the way some women would have. Instead, she flushed redder and looked down.

He nudged her arm. "What did I say wrong?"

"I don't know. I'm just so awkward. With a

man who's, you know, attractive." She didn't look at him.

He had to think a minute before he realized what she was saying. "You mean, you're awkward with me?"

She nodded miserably.

Happiness surged through him. Sweet, pure Hannah was thinking of him as a man. Not just a friend or a coworker, but the kind of man she found attractive. Wasn't that what she'd said?

With an effort, he tamped down his feelings, because he didn't want to embarrass her more. "Is this what we talked about before?" he asked gently. "How you're uncomfortable with the opposite sex, in a dating way?"

She nodded and then lifted both hands like stop signs. "Not that we're dating or anything! I didn't mean to imply that." She rolled her eyes a little, as if annoyed with herself.

"No, but...if you feel that way, do you want to talk about it? Maybe I can help." It wasn't a line. He really wanted to help this struggling woman toward happiness. He wasn't quite sure *why* he wanted that so badly, but he did.

She tilted her head to one side, reminding him of a curious sparrow who might fly off if he moved too quickly. "How could you help?"

He shrugged. "Maybe...just try talking to me

normally. The same way you'd talk to a man on a date. With practice, it'll get easier."

She narrowed her eyes, studying him. "Like you were with Bridget?" she asked.

"Like I… How was I with Bridget?"

She waved a hand. "Just…flirty. Sophisticated, in a way I'll never be."

There was so much to say here, so much to think about, and yet he had to tread lightly. Something had changed in how Hannah looked at him, and he was pretty sure he liked it. A lot. He didn't want to stop it before it began.

He caught her hand in his, squeezed it lightly. "Touch, like that? It's part of flirting," he said. It was just a demonstration, but he found he had to force himself to let go.

Especially when he noticed that her breathing had quickened. Another surge flashed through him. His touch affected her. Which was a heady thing, even if ultimately, a woman like Hannah would never go for a Hutchenson.

She pushed her hair behind one ear.

"That's good!" he said. "That's something women do when they're flirting. They play with their hair."

"I didn't mean to—"

"It's unconscious. But it lets the guy know, on some level, that you're interested."

She looked at him, her eyes full of vulnerable

emotion. "I feel silly," she said. "I feel like a silly girl. And…" Her forehead wrinkled. "I don't mean to promise something I'm never going to deliver."

"We're just talking," he assured her. "Nothing you said would make me expect anything from you."

"Some men do," she said, her voice low and bleak.

He clasped her hand in both of his, studying her unhappy face, anger starting to simmer in him. "Did something happen?"

She looked away, pulled away. "Kind of."

"Do you want to talk about it?"

A rapid shake of the head.

"I'm a good listener."

She stared at the floor. "It's just… I showed interest in someone and he thought that meant he could do whatever he wanted. Called me a tease when I backed away. So I… I guess I'm scared to give somebody the wrong idea."

He so wanted to pull her into his arms. He did go so far as to put an arm along the back of her chair, just in a brotherly way.

But when she looked over at him, awareness flashed in her eyes.

Luke wasn't one of those guys who thought every glance from a woman meant she was interested in him. He'd always been a little cautious; he'd wanted to be sure before he made a move, because the idea of pushing himself on a woman made him feel sick.

There was no doubt about it, though, with Hannah. She was interested on some level.

He didn't want her to feel bad about that, or wrong. Even though it couldn't go anywhere between them.

He leaned closer and let his hand skim through a lock of her hair. Soft and fine and such a light blond; she'd stayed a towhead.

She met his eyes again, for a little longer, and then looked away. A voice over the hospital speaker announced a code blue. A doctor stuck her head in, looked around and then left.

And Luke remembered where he was, and what he was doing. He was in a hospital waiting to see his father, who'd gotten himself here largely due to his own issues with drinking.

Hannah was a fantastic person, smart and hardworking and really, really pretty, but she was naive about love. She'd gotten a little bit attracted to Luke, but it didn't mean anything. Didn't mean he was right for her or that it would work.

It was up to him to keep things cool between them.

He pulled away his hand, took his arm from around her shoulders. "And that's flirting," he said, hoping he was convincingly playing the role of a benevolent teacher. "Actually, you're not bad at it."

Which came out more flirtatious than fatherly.

He needed to find another topic. "I think I'm going to take Dad to see Bobby, at the prison. Once he recovers enough to go."

Hannah's eyes widened and she scooted away in her chair. "Really? Oh…wow."

So much for flirting, being drawn to him. All of a sudden, she seemed repulsed.

And why wouldn't she be? *She* didn't have family members in jail. She wasn't a Hutchenson, or anything like a Hutchenson.

He needed to remember that, and forget about how soft her hair felt, how pretty her flushed face looked. He needed to think of her as a colleague and nothing else. "Did you bring work for me to do?" he asked. "I'll be spending some time in the waiting room today and for the next few days. If there's planning to be done, maybe I can work from here."

"Right. Of course." She reached for her laptop bag.

There. Back to business. He hoped.

Hannah pulled out her laptop, trying to pretend Luke hadn't just rocked her world.

When she'd gotten his text, she'd rushed over

here on the pretext of checking in on him and bringing him cookies, but really, because she was so eager to see him. She'd acted like a fool at Cleo's, running off, and she'd wanted to get back to normal.

She'd been pushing aside the fact that she thought he was incredibly handsome and that she was getting more and more drawn to him. But when he'd explained his behavior with the clerk at Cleo's as just flirting, when he'd taken it upon himself to show *her* how to do it…she'd been floored. Stunned. Silenced.

He'd put his arm around her and he'd touched her hair, and it had felt wonderful.

Being single and not dating, Hannah never— but never—got that kind of tender touch. And from a man like Luke, a man she admired and felt for, it had been the most special and amazing moment.

She'd even thought, ever so briefly, that he was going to kiss her.

Would she have let him? Right there in the surgery waiting room at the hospital?

Well…yes. Yes, she probably would have let him, she had to admit to herself.

And then he'd brought up his brother. He was going to take his dad to visit his brother in prison.

Which was great, of course. Bobby surely needed visitors and to reconnect with his family.

But Hannah wasn't sure how much Bobby knew about Marnie and the twins. Marnie had said she hadn't told him, but what if he'd somehow found out? If someone mentioned that Hannah was raising Marnie's twins, couldn't he do the math?

The whole thing left her sick with dread, unsure of whether she was doing the right thing. She'd impulsively agreed to Marnie's condition, and she'd started down the road of keeping the twins' parentage a secret, but was that viable? Was it right?

And what would happen if Luke and his father learned that the twins were a part of their family, and that Hannah had been keeping the connection a secret?

They weren't going to be happy.

She needed to minimize her connection to Luke and stick to business if she was going to have a chance of keeping her promise to Marnie.

Chapter Eight

On Wednesday after work, Hannah drove toward home, the twins in the back seat, and tried not to be nervous that Luke was in the front seat beside her.

"I really appreciate this," he said. His car hadn't started this morning, and he'd walked the three miles to Rescue Haven.

Of course, Hannah had insisted on driving him home. What else could she do? It was cold outside, spitting snow, and he was her next-door neighbor.

"I hate to ask another favor," he said, "but could you stop by Pasquale's Pizza on the way?"

"No problem." She took a left and drove the two blocks to the only non-chain pizza place in Bethlehem Springs.

He jumped out, and she turned back to check on the twins, trying not to watch Luke as he headed into the shop. He was good-looking, of course. Kind, and appreciative, and strong. And he had the slightest swagger in his walk that was masculine and appealing.

But because he intended to visit his brother, she needed to keep her distance. The fewer chances she had to spill the beans about Bobby being the twins' father, the better.

He came out of the pizza shop quickly—he must have called ahead—carrying a big flat box and a white bag. What would it be like if this was a family scenario, if they were Mom and Dad and kids, stopping for takeout on the way home from work?

She couldn't help it. Her chest filled with longing.

He climbed into her small car, juggling the large flat box to make it fit without encroaching on the gearshift.

She had to laugh at the size of his meal. "Hungry?"

"Are you?" He opened the box a little, and the rich, garlicky fragrance of Pasquale's special sauce filled the car.

Her stomach growled, loudly.

"Pee-zah!" Addie shouted from the back seat.

"Peez!" Emmy added, almost as loud.

"That's just cruel," she said as she pulled the car back onto the road and steered toward Luke's place. "You're tempting us. I may have to order some when I get these girls home."

"No, you won't," he said. "This is for all of us. The least I can do is feed you, after you drove me around."

Her stomach gave a little leap, and not just about the prospect of pizza. Why was he inviting her to have dinner with him? Was there an ulterior motive? And if there was, would she mind? "We shouldn't," she said, and then cleared her throat to get the breathless sound out of her voice. "Mom's expecting us."

"Invite your mom over," he urged, which made it sound like just a friendly invitation. That was mostly a relief.

"She *would* probably welcome the chance not to cook for us," Hannah said. "Especially since she said she has a bunch of paperwork, and she usually spreads it out all over the kitchen table."

"Good, we'll eat here. Although Dad definitely doesn't have high chairs lying around." He frowned, then snapped his fingers. "I know. We'll put a blanket on the kitchen floor and have a picnic. And Goldie will clean up the floor afterward."

She swallowed. That sounded sweet, a dream come true. She forced her thoughts away from romance, forced herself to think about his dad's house and to remember what a mess it had been. They'd definitely want to put down a blanket, and watch the girls carefully, too. But she couldn't make herself decline the invitation. "Okay, then, we'll come," she said.

"Good." He proceeded to turn around and entertain the babies with tickling and silly faces and talk of pizza until she pulled in to his gravel driveway.

She sent a quick text to her mother and then got out of the car to find that Luke was already unfastening Emmy. He swung her comfortably into the crook of his arm and then grabbed the pizza box and bag. He waited while she unfastened Addie, and when she went to pick up the heavy diaper bag, he took it from her and shrugged it onto his shoulder.

Yeah, it would definitely be nice to have a partner when raising twins.

She held the storm door for him, and when they got inside, she looked around in amazement. Gone were the stacks of magazines, the clutter of mail and boxes, the dust and dirt. The couch was covered with a throw, and a recliner looked brand-new. Aside from a couple of small end tables and a TV, the room was bare, with vacuum lines still showing in the old shag carpet. "Oh, Luke, it looks like a different place!"

"Much needed," he said, "and since Dad's staying at the hospital another couple of nights, I've had time."

She set down Emmy to toddle around and Luke did the same with Addie, and then they both did a quick sweep of the room to lift anything dangerous out of reach. "Where'd you learn to clean?" she asked. "I might invite you over to take a stab at Mom's place."

"Army," he said, moving a big dog chew just as Addie reached for it. "I think everything's safe now. I'll grab a blanket and let Goldie out. She's staying in the garage," he clarified. "It's my compromise with Dad. I think it's too cold for her outside, but he doesn't want her in the house."

"Got it. But you'll bring her in after?"

"Sure." He grinned. "You love her, don't you?"

She nodded. She loved all dogs, but Goldie was special. Maybe because she and Luke had basically saved the young dog's life.

While Luke dealt with Goldie, she strolled through the place, marveling at the changes he'd made. Even the windows seemed to have been washed—no easy feat at this time of year. She peeked into the kitchen and noted that every surface shone.

He came back in, Goldie leashed at his side, and spread a blanket on the floor. He let Goldie sniff the girls and then tied her long leash to a heavy chair. When he ordered her to lie down, she immediately complied.

"Nice!" Hannah clapped her hands. "You've been working with her."

"A lot," he admitted. "It's my main activity, aside from work and the cleanup. And it's fun. She learns fast."

"You're doing a great job." She meant it, too. Luke had a bit of a reputation in town, for drinking and rabble-rousing and generally being irresponsible, but he was proving it to be unfounded. Or maybe he'd changed. Either way, she was impressed with him.

He brought out plates while Hannah filled the twins' sippy cups with water, and they settled on the blanket in front of a small gas heater. Luke opened the pizza box and the white bag. "I got bread sticks, plain ones. I didn't know if Addie and Emmy liked pizza, although it sounds like they're familiar."

"As long as I cut it up small, it's okay. Honestly, we have it at least once a week, and Pasquale's is our favorite, too."

Hannah's phone buzzed. It was Mom, saying she'd finish up some paperwork and come over. Good. That would nix any romantic vibes or notions that might crop up between them.

With the twins rapturously gobbling tiny pieces of pizza, Hannah and Luke ate at a more leisurely pace, talking about the project at work, his dad and the twins. Halfway through the meal,

Luke put on a playlist of quiet, jazzy Christmas carols. Once the twins were finished, Hannah wiped down their hands and Luke found some wooden spoons and pans for them to bang on. Clearly, he'd remembered that drumming was a favorite activity.

As Luke wrapped the remaining pizza and Hannah washed the plates, she felt him looking at her. She glanced over, raising an eyebrow, but he just smiled and put the pizza into the fridge.

Heat rose in Hannah's chest. Why had he looked at her that way? Was it part of the flirting behavior he'd tried to explain to her at the hospital, or was he just being friendly? Was he liking the domesticity of the evening as much as she was?

Dangerous. "I don't know where Mom is," she said, her voice a little squeaky.

He walked back over to where she was standing. "You okay?" he asked as he wiped the counter.

He was at a perfectly respectable distance, not touching her, so why did she feel so warm?

Goldie barked, and there was a knock on the door. Luke gave Hannah a quick, curious glance and then went to open it.

Mom came bustling in and the moment was over.

"We saved you some pizza," he said to Mom.

"Gamma!" Emmy lifted her arms, while Addie rushed to Mom and hugged her legs.

Mom kneeled between the two. "You're getting so heavy! And what's this? Have you got a drum?" She tapped on one of the pots Luke had found, which led to both girls beating loudly on them.

Mom stood up and beckoned to Luke. "I wasn't sure this would be appropriate, but I think it is. I have something for you, but you'll have to help me bring it in." She led the way out to the car while Hannah wondered what Mom had up her sleeve. Probably bakery goods.

But she was wrong. Mom and Luke returned, each carrying large plastic storage containers. Mom set them down in the middle of the floor. "Christmas decorations," she said, sounding out of breath. "I have so many, and we've already decorated as much as we can with the girls so small. I thought it might cheer up your dad when he came home if the house was decorated."

Luke studied the boxes, then looked back at Mom. "I don't know what to say. I... After what Dad did at Thanksgiving, you're offering us your decorations to cheer him up?"

"He's had struggles," Mom said simply. "I understand that." She walked over to the girls. "Now, I'm going to take these tired young ladies home. Hannah, you stay and help Luke decorate."

Hannah frowned. "I thought you were staying for pizza."

"I'll take a piece home. Honestly, I can't wait to get them bathed and to bed, then put on my pj's and read my book."

It *sounded* legit, but Hannah looked at her mom suspiciously. Was she purposely pushing Hannah and Luke together?

But there was no stopping this train. Mom put jackets on the girls, and Luke helped her get them into her car, while Hannah stood in the middle of the kitchen, left to her dangerous attraction.

As he came back inside, Luke remembered all the old urges.

A woman, in a good mood, in a house alone. Both of them unattached.

The old Luke knew exactly what to do in that situation. But this was Hannah, and he was a different person now. A man of faith, a man who honored women.

He couldn't entirely forget what he knew. He'd seen the way Hannah looked at him. She wasn't immune to the feelings that sparked between them.

He wouldn't consider acting on those feelings, though. Even if he hadn't felt protective due to their shared past, and even if he hadn't been a changed man, there was what her mother had said. After they'd gotten the twins into the car, as he'd been turning back to the house, she'd stepped in front of him and given him a look that was, he imagined, a look most mothers knew how to give. "You take care of my daughter," she'd said, staring hard at him. Implied: *you know exactly what I mean.*

He'd nodded and said, "Of course." It had felt like a bit of a vow.

He walked into the living room, looked at Hannah standing there, so pretty and kissable and completely unaware of it, and brushed his hands together. His old ways had been tamped down, but were not entirely gone. He really wanted to pull her into his arms. Instead, he cleared his throat and spoke abruptly. "So. I guess we need to get to work."

"Hey." Hannah's voice sounded small, and she looked at the ground. "If you don't want to decorate or you don't want me here…"

He didn't need to act like a jerk to keep his hands to himself. He was old enough and man enough to be respectful. "No, I do," he said, forcing friend vibrations into his voice. "Come on, let's look at what your mom brought."

"If you're sure…"

"I'm sure." He kneeled beside the bigger container, opened it and stared blankly at the jumble inside. "I definitely need help figuring out how to deal with all this."

"How to deal with it?" She opened the other container. "Not much for decorating?"

"Look around you," he said, waving a hand at the blank walls. "I can clean, but decorating is something else."

"You never put up a tree?" she asked, looking incredulous.

He had a sudden memory of decorating a tree with Nicolette and her mom when they'd first gotten together. It had, in fact, been a first for him, since they'd never decorated growing up. They'd had a good time, especially with Nicolette clapping her hands to see the colorful lights and shiny ornaments.

Tonight would be different in all kinds of ways. Rather than talking about it, he changed the subject. "Strings of lights. Do they work?" He pulled out a big tangle and took them over to one of the outlets. They all lit up, in various colors.

"We did white lights at Mom's this year," she said, "so looks like you get the colored ones. You okay with that?"

"Why wouldn't I be? They're pretty. And beggars can't be choosers." He looked around the room, then back at Hannah. "Problem is, I don't have a tree. So how do we put them up?"

"We'll figure something out." She patted his arm. "Let's see what else is here and then we'll decide."

What was it about women that got them all happy around holidays and decorating? He didn't exactly share the feeling, but being here with Hannah was fun. She had him wind garland around the banister, then stepped back and studied it, frowned and made him move it from one side of the staircase to the other. She rummaged through Dad's cupboards until she found a white bowl, then she filled it with ornaments and set it on the coffee table. She made him hunt down pushpins—who would have guessed Dad would have those?—and climbed up on a stool to string the colored lights around the upper corners of the room.

When she swayed, he hurried over to steady her. "I should be the one climbing around," he said.

"I'm fine. I know what I'm doing. Hold these." She handed him the rest of the lights, climbed down and moved the stool over. Then she climbed back up, took the lights from him and continued stringing them around the room.

He stood beside the stool and handed her pushpins, then steadied her when she overreached. Actually, he was just fine with playing a supporting role.

Fine with being close to her.

They sorted through the rest of the ornaments and statues—a Mickey Mouse that lifted its hands and recited "Merry Christmas," a couple of candles and a stuffed Santa made to perch on the edge of a table or hearth. He set that one on the end table, then frowned. "If Goldie gets in here, she'll think that's a toy," he said.

"Good point. Maybe put it on the mantel." She frowned. "You know, this is going to be a bit of a job to take down. How long do you think you'll stay in Bethlehem Springs?"

"Good question." He leaned back against the couch. "Until Dad can manage on his own, obviously. After that... I don't know. There's lots to consider."

She started untangling the last string of lights. "Like what?"

"Whether we can get the new structure ready to go so I have a full-time job, that's one," he said. "Also..." He trailed off, because he didn't want to burden her.

"What?" she asked. Her face was kind, open. "What's bothering you?"

He sighed. "It's being a Hutchenson in Bethlehem Springs," he said. "We're the family everyone tries to stay away from. Makes it hard to get a fresh start."

"I know what you mean, but most people

aren't judging. Everyone has problems of their own. Oh…" She'd been digging through one of the tubs and she pulled out something small and blue. "Mom must have left this in here by mistake. I know she'd never get rid of it."

"What is it?" He held out a hand. "Can I see?"

She swallowed hard and placed the object into his hand.

It was a flat piece of plaster, with a small handprint, painted bright blue. Around the bottom, MARNIE A. was carved in capital letters. The disc hung on a red ribbon. Probably supposed to be put on a Christmas tree.

He handed it back to Hannah, and she stared at it, her eyes shiny with tears.

The urge to comfort her physically was strong, but he didn't. "Put it somewhere safe," he said. "It's a keeper."

She wrapped it back up in newspaper and tucked it into her purse. Then she found a tissue and blew her nose.

Poor kid. She'd lost her big sister, and here she was raising her sister's daughters, getting reminded of her loss every day. And it was Christmas.

He was just about to pull her into a friendly hug when she took a big step away from him, pulled a Christmas tablecloth out of the box, carried it to Dad's rickety dining table and draped it over. Then she dug out a fat red candle and holder and set it in the middle of the table. "There! You'll have more cheerful meals now."

"Uh-huh." He didn't really see him and his dad sitting down to home-cooked meals at a table.

"So," she said, still sounding brisk as she took a roll of red ribbon out of the box, "what was the army like? How long were you in?"

It was a clear effort to keep the conversation away from Marnie and loss and sadness, but that was understandable. "Ten years," he said, "and it was…the army." What more could he say? He hadn't hated it, but he hadn't loved it, either. It had been a living.

"Were you overseas?" She strung the ribbon through the greenery along the banister.

"Part of the time I was stateside, but yeah. I spent some years in Iraq."

"Did it leave an impact?"

"Hard to say." How much did she know about his past? he wondered. He busied himself with unwrapping what turned out to be a small, pre-decorated artificial tree. "I never really thought I was affected by the years in the military—" he said, and broke off. And then, looking at her good-listener face, he figured he might as well tell it all. "I did get pretty screwed up when I came home," he said, "but that was to do with Bobby, too."

Her face tightened, just like it did every time he mentioned his brother. *Why?* He decided to push it. "You didn't really know him, did you?"

"No!" She said it abruptly. "I mean, I knew him, just like you know everyone around here, but we weren't friends. He was more friends with Marnie." She grabbed the little tree he'd found, plugged it in and tried to straighten out the branches.

She didn't look at him.

Maybe mentioning Bobby brought up sad memories of Marnie, since they'd been friends. "I remember Bobby and Marnie were close for a while." They'd shared an interest in trouble, that was why.

She frowned, stood and set the tree on an end table. "So...you were saying you got screwed up? What happened? If that's not too nosy of a question."

He shrugged. "I can tell it if you want to hear it."

"I do. I'm curious." Then she flushed like she'd said something revealing.

She'd definitely gotten jumpy, nervous. The happy holiday mood was gone, so he might as well tell her his sad-sack story. "Being in the army, I got into some drinking. When I came home, it escalated."

"To the point where it was a problem?"

He shrugged. "Kind of. I kept control because I didn't want to be like Dad, but I definitely drank too much." He flashed back to an evening he'd come home drunk while Nicki was still awake. The confusion in her eyes had stopped him cold, and he'd quit drinking immediately.

That had lasted until the breakup. Without Nicki's sweet innocence to hold him to a higher standard, he'd gone straight downhill.

No need to go into the worst of the details. "I had some bad times," he said, "and I ended up at a mission for the homeless in Cleveland."

She looked puzzled. "Working there?"

He had, eventually. He could just say yes. *Tell the truth.* "All of us who lived there did some chores."

"You…lived at a mission?"

He focused on straightening up the remaining decorations, stacking them neatly in one of the containers. "For a couple of months. They helped me a lot. But…just not in time."

"Oh, Luke." She reached for his arm, squeezed it and then wrapped her arms around her knees, not even pretending to focus on decorating. "What do you mean 'not in time'?"

"The main reason I wanted to get my life together was to help Bobby," he said. "But by the time I was healthy enough to seek him out, he was on trial." He swallowed hard, made himself say the rest. "For felony murder. He didn't pull the trigger himself, but he was right there, participating in the armed robbery, when his buddy went nuts and shot the cashier." He'd been in the courtroom when Mrs. Singh had made her victim statement, shown the jury pictures of the three school-age children she'd now be raising alone.

If only he'd gotten it together in time to stop Bobby's downhill slide. Luke was the big brother. Bobby might have listened to him.

Hannah scrambled to her feet. "That's awful, Luke, I'm so sorry." She pulled her phone out of her back pocket. "Look at the time. I have to get home."

He pulled his mind out of the past and looked at her blankly. She was so kind and understanding, a wonderful Christian. But any mention of Bobby seemed to send her running.

Not that he blamed her. What Bobby had done had resulted in a man's death, had devastated a family.

He knew from experience that going down that rabbit hole of shame and anger and grief would do him no good. He stood and looked around the room, purposely pushing away the past and focusing on the present moment, on the Christmas decorations they'd put up. The room was actually looking good.

"I can walk you home," he said.

"No, I have the car, remember?" She was grabbing her parka from the hook on the back of the door.

He moved across the room to hold it for her, but she stepped away.

A brush-off. Clear enough. "Get some rest," he said as she scuttled out the door. "We really have to put in the hours tomorrow if we want to catch up."

As he closed the door behind her, he couldn't stop thinking about her reaction to hearing Bobby's name. She didn't seem put off or disapproving; she seemed scared. But why?

Chapter Nine

The next day, Hannah walked through a cold drizzle into the old barn, now dog-training-area-in-progress. She was a woman with a goal.

She intended to do her work today and stay distant from Luke. Cool. Friendly, but not too friendly. No repeat of the emotional roller coaster of last night.

Decorating Luke's dad's house with him had felt domestic and warm and wonderful. Even when he'd told her about his past mistakes, she had compared it to the man he was now and admired him for all he'd done to repair his life. There was no doubt he'd come from a disadvantaged past, full of poverty and neglect and maybe even abuse from his dad. No wonder he'd slipped and fallen. She was impressed that he'd gotten back up.

And then he'd mentioned Bobby. After that,

being impressed and admiring had seemed like a big, major mistake. One she kept making.

Today would be different. Mom had kept the twins home today, planning to take them to an appointment with a pediatric developmentalist for some testing, so she didn't even have the small distraction of dropping them off or wondering how they were doing at day care. She'd focus entirely on her work. Not on Addie and Emmy, and definitely not on Luke.

She put down her coat, grabbed her clipboard and studied her to-do list. She had to source some used bleachers and help Luke measure heights for a couple of jump sets. They had to cut PVC for the weave poles, and though he'd seen them once at the facility they'd visited, she needed to find him some pictures to work with.

That should keep them busy and focused and nonromantic.

Luke walked in, and her heart did a big, hard flip.

He'd revealed a lot of himself last night, his background, the trauma of what Bobby had done. She'd seen in his demeanor that he thought the stories would turn her off, but they'd had the opposite effect; they'd given her sympathy, made her admire him more.

Now, seeing his rough morning face, she

wanted nothing more than to go to him, ask him how he'd slept, give him a hug. Girlfriend things.

She drew a line through the tasks she'd planned to do with him, put initials by the ones they'd each do alone. She couldn't keep her distance while working closely together. It didn't make sense.

But it also didn't make sense to avoid the work they were being paid to do so that she wouldn't be uncomfortable. Reluctantly, she erased the cross-outs.

"What's on deck for today?" he asked as he came over to where she was standing. He slung his coat carelessly on a chair. That smile...

Her heart beating hard, she turned away, scanned her list and focused on individual tasks. "You need to get the walls framed up," she said, keeping her voice businesslike. "I have some equipment to order."

He finished his job in less than an hour and approached her again.

She took a big step back.

Crossing his arms over his chest, he frowned at her. "What's going on?"

"Nothing!" She looked around, grabbed her trusty clipboard. "I'm just stressed out, that's all. It's important to me to get this done so I can have a job with insurance." She realized how selfish she sounded. How selfish she was being. "So we both can," she added quickly, although for Luke to get a permanent job here meant he'd continue living next door to the twins indefinitely, unaware that he was their uncle.

His eyes narrowed, and he tilted his head to one side. He wasn't going to buy it. He was going to make her talk to him about what was wrong, and what could she say?

Then, to her relief, he shrugged and lifted his hands, palms up. "That's important to me, too. What's next?"

Focused on a goal, they worked together for the rest of the day. Reese stopped in at lunchtime, bringing hoagies and bags of chips from a sandwich shop. "I didn't want you to have to slow down," he explained. "Our benefactors want to visit next week."

That lit a fire under them, and they worked silently and efficiently through the afternoon, laying artificial turf over a big section of flooring and tacking it down. She showed him a video of weave poles and then held the PVC pipes while he cut them to the right length. Dimly, she heard car doors slamming in the distance; the day-care kids were getting picked up.

"Can you stay late?" she asked him. "Mom has the twins, so I can."

"I have nothing else to do, at least until Dad comes home. Let's keep working."

They were so busy setting up the equipment that time passed quickly. Finally, well after sunset, they took a break.

They leaned back against the wooden wall of the single old stall they'd left in place, intending to finish it as an office. He handed her a soda from the cooler he'd brought, then took one for himself.

Perspiration dripped down the back of Hannah's neck. She took a long draw and fanned herself. "Hot work," she said.

Luke held his cold can against her cheek. "That should cool you off."

"Don't," she said, and scooted away, because the act felt too intimate. Then she stared miserably at the floorboards. Awkward Hannah. That was all she'd ever be.

She waited for his criticism, but it didn't come. Finally, she hazarded a glance in his direction. Just as she'd feared, he was studying her. She shook her head, making her hair fall to shield her face.

"Want to tell me what's wrong?" he asked quietly.

The thing was, she *did* want to tell him. To tell him that he was the most attractive man she'd ever been around, and that she was feeling more emotions toward him every day. To tell him that he made her comfortable enough to want to explore that world of dating and men she'd shunned for so long.

That he was the uncle of the twins, and that his brother was their father.

But that, she couldn't say.

She scrambled to her feet. "I'll be back, I just... I just have to get something out of my car." It was a weak excuse, but she didn't stay long enough for him to question it. She hurried to the barn door, opened it and walked out into a mix of freezing rain and snow.

As she headed toward her car, not sure whether she'd go back inside or just drive away—*run away*—her feet started to go out from under her and she windmilled her arms to keep from going down.

She ran her foot back and forth over the paved driveway. Ice.

Solid and hard, for how fast it must have frozen. Reese hadn't said anything about ice when he'd come in. But then that had been hours ago.

She walked the rest of the way to her car, carefully. It, too, was encased in a thin shell of ice.

When she tried the door, it didn't move. Frozen shut.

She could work on it, probably get it open, but she wasn't so sure about driving home. The rolling country roads out this way didn't tend to get treated quickly, especially when the workday was over and people were mostly safe at home.

She sucked in a breath of static-smelling, icy air and headed back to the barn. Pushing open the door, she walked inside.

Luke was back to work, fitting PVC poles together.

"We're in trouble," she called to him.

"Oh?" His hands stilled and he looked over his shoulder at her.

She gestured back toward the door. "Ice storm."

As if on cue, the lights went out.

The barn was as pitch-black as a deep cave. Feeling his way with his feet, Luke walked toward the spot where Hannah was standing. "Where are you?"

"Luke?" she said at the same time. Her hand caught one of his.

His other hand, reaching toward her, brushed against her hair. Just like the one time he'd touched it before, it was soft and silky. His hand wanted to linger. The black darkness intensified everything, enclosing them in a world of their own.

She'd gone still, holding his other hand.

Kiss her! You'd be crazy not to kiss her!

It was his old self speaking. He pulled back both hands and cleared his throat. "You stay here," he said. "I'm going to see how bad it is." *And cool off.*

He felt his way to the door and went out into the darkness, sucking in air. Wind whipped around him, penetrating his flannel shirt, freezing his sweat. It looked like the ice storm had turned into a snowstorm, or at least a squall. Visibility was practically zero. He tested his footing because of what Hannah had said.

Yep. Ice underneath the blowing, deepening snow.

He went back inside on a snowy gust and pushed hard to close the door behind him. "Turned into a squall," he said. "Probably won't last long, but for now, visibility is basically zero. Better get comfortable." He pushed aside the burlap curtain that covered the barn's big sash window, and a little gray light filtered in.

Now he could see Hannah's face, and she looked panicky. Clearly, she'd felt what sparked between them. "I'll call Gabby," she said. "Maybe we can make it up to the house and hang out with them."

Was it that bad, being stuck here with just him?

From her frantic scrolling of her phone, apparently it was.

Relief crossed her face when Gabby answered. They spoke for a few minutes, Hannah's face becoming steadily less cheerful. She nodded, frowned and ended the call. "They're all up at the church tonight, doing that craft workshop," she said. "Izzy and Gabby's grandma, too. They're hunkering down there until the roads get treated. She didn't say anything about a squall."

"Probably didn't hit them yet."

She hesitated, then spoke again. "She did say we'd be better off to stay here than to try to walk up to the house. It's all locked up, and they don't leave a key out."

"Makes sense," he said gravely. So they were stuck here, and he tamped down an exultant feeling, another one straight from his past. When they got out of this situation, he was going to make an appointment with the pastor. He was supposed to be a new, cleansed man, so why were his old urges still so strong?

"Guess we should make ourselves comfortable," he said.

She still looked panicky.

"Don't worry, you're safe with me." He said it firmly, meeting and holding her gaze, so she'd get that he wasn't going to try anything, make a move. The last thing he wanted was for her to be afraid of him.

Her cheeks went pink and she studied his face. Wow, she was pretty.

"Okay," she said, and then shivered. "I'm cold."

He looked around for his coat and tried to give it to her, but she held up a hand. "No, Luke, you need to stay warm, too."

"That's going to be a problem, depending on how long this storm lasts," he said. "The space heaters cut off right along with the lights."

Her eyes widened. "What are we going to do?"

"Body heat," he joked automatically, and then could have kicked himself. How was she going to trust him when he said things like that?

She nodded. "I guess that's what we'll have to do."

She'd taken him seriously. *Uh-oh.*

His expression must have showed his discomfort.

"Unless you don't want to," she said, sounding shy.

"It's just for a little while." He hoped. Sometimes outages around here lasted all night, or at least, they had when he was a kid.

He stepped closer and saw that she was shivering. "C'mere," he said. He tucked her beneath his arm and urged her toward the wall where they'd been sitting before. "Sit here and I'll keep you warm."

He tended to run hot. Women had always liked that about him.

Might as well use it for a good cause.

They sat down together and he spread his coat over them. They shifted around to get comfortable and she nestled in.

His heart rate shot up.

He inhaled the surprisingly spicy scent of her. He'd never have pegged Hannah for wearing fancy perfume, but she smelled really, really good.

She fit perfectly beneath his arm, against his side.

They sat like that for a little while, not talking. Wind whipped around the old barn, making it creak. Inside, together, though, they were warm.

He liked it too much. Not just in the old physical way, but something different. He wanted to protect Hannah, to keep her warm in all kinds of ways. Wanted to help her feel safe and secure. Wanted to reassure her.

It was a feeling he'd never had before, a feeling of being responsible for a woman's well-being. It seemed to make his heart swell in his chest. The fact that he wasn't angling to make things physical, had no intention of it, buoyed him up and made him feel like a better man.

"Luke?" Her voice was tentative.

"Yeah?" He looked down at her, pulled her closer. "Still cold?"

"No, I…" She raised an eyebrow. "You know how you said I was safe with you?"

"I meant it."

She nodded and relaxed into him, turning a bit, her hand on his arm now. She probably didn't realize she was stroking his arm, just lightly.

He looked down at her, and when she shivered, he tucked the jacket closer around her.

She reached up and touched his face. "You need to shave," she said, running a finger over his stubbly cheek.

"I do." He caught her hand as it started to tangle in his hair, squeezed it and moved it down to her own lap.

"Sorry," she whispered, so softly he had to lean down to hear.

"Don't be sorry. I'm not."

Their gazes met and held for a long moment and then she looked away.

He let the side of his face rest on top of her head for a moment and breathed slowly. He'd promised she'd be safe, and that had given her the courage to explore.

Here came her hand again, reaching for his arm, stroking it.

He reached for it, held it in front of him and, one at a time, tucked her fingers down until her hand was a loose fist in front of him. "You're safe with me," he said, hearing the strain in his own voice, "but I'm not a robot. Being close to you, it's…it affects me."

She shifted to face him. "I know. Me, too." She looked at him steadily now.

He leaned forward to see her better, her fisted hand an inch away from his mouth. "What do you want?"

She bit her lip. "I don't know."

He drew in a slow breath and let it out just as slowly. Then he pulled her hand to him and dropped a kiss on each knuckle, never looking away from her.

Her hand was so tiny in his. Not soft—she worked hard—but tiny.

He breathed in, breathed out. Watched her eyes and saw them darken. Looked at that beautiful mouth.

"This is…tough," he said, barely managing to get the words out.

She looked into his eyes. "Not easy for me, either." The words were as quiet as a feather brushing his ear.

She rose up to her knees, leaned toward him and put her hands on his shoulders. Then she pressed her lips to his.

He cupped her face and let her kiss him, the action tentative and unsure, just a brief touch of lips. That was fine. This was going to be okay.

He'd keep his hands still, right where they were, and it would be over, and he could breathe.

She closed her eyes and did it again, slower, lingering.

He stiffened and stayed utterly still.

She pulled back and tilted her head to one side. "Don't you like it?" she asked.

That made him laugh a little. "Oh, Hannah."

One of her eyebrows lifted. "Yeah?"

All of a sudden, he wondered if she might know exactly what she was doing. He let his hand stray into her hair, to brush into the softness of it.

She turned her face into his hand and kissed it, closing her eyes.

He closed his, too. *I really tried, Lord.*

And then he gathered her close and kissed her the way it seemed like she needed to be kissed.

Chapter Ten

Hannah's heart raced as Luke's lips pressed hers, quick and hard. She pulled back to look at him, half scared, half wanting to memorize this moment.

His arms, warm around her, made her feel more secure and grounded than she could ever remember.

He touched her cheek. "This okay?"

It was a genuine question. He was asking for her consent. For the briefest moment, she flashed back to the time when she hadn't been asked, and her muscles tensed.

Deliberately, she relaxed them and focused on Luke: his strong arms, his gentle touch, the concern in his eyes. "More than okay," she whispered.

"Then close your eyes." It was half request, half order.

The last thing she saw was his intent, warm gaze. Then she closed her eyes and her other senses blossomed to life: the firm, absolutely confident pressure of his lips; the scent of him, some masculine, foresty soap; the sound of her own indrawn breath.

She'd never been kissed like this. Never been *held* like this, and the comfort of it melted something that had been frozen inside her since she'd been a young teenager.

It wasn't something he was doing *to* her; she was a full participant. When she pulled back a little, afraid she was showing too much enthusiasm, he stroked her hair and she felt him smile against her mouth and knew it was good, that she wanted to be nowhere else but right here, doing this exact thing, and she was pretty sure he felt the same way.

Minutes later, a sound intruded. From outside, a harsh, repetitive scraping.

She pulled back. "What's that?"

"Plows are here," he said. "They're scraping and salting the roads." He listened. "Could be a power truck out there, too."

So they *weren't* stuck. They didn't have to stay here, in the darkness, kissing.

She reached up and ran a finger over his bristly cheek. She breathed in the scent of him.

They didn't have to stay here, but she didn't want to leave. She leaned against him, wrapped her arms around that strong, muscular chest.

After a minute, he took gentle hold of her wrists and moved her hands away from him. "We should get ready to go."

She couldn't help the small, resistant sound she made. She didn't want this to end.

When she opened her eyes, he was looking at her, his expression serious. What did *that* mean? That he wasn't as into it as she'd been?

He pulled her close against his chest and kissed the top of her head, and she felt again that delicious security, but another doubt rushed in behind it: had she led him on? As she'd been accused of doing that awful time before?

There was a quiet snap, and the lights flashed on.

And here she was, practically sitting in Luke's lap. Obviously enjoying his embrace. Which, whether it meant that she was a tease who led men on, or whether it had been a pity kiss, or whether he wanted it to be the start of something more, the upshot was the same: she shouldn't have let it happen. Feeling horribly exposed, she scrambled to her feet.

Kissing Luke Hutchenson had been a big mistake that could only lead in a direction she couldn't possibly go.

* * *

After the delightful surprise of kissing Hannah, Luke's life crashed back into its everyday reality when he brought his father home from the hospital Saturday morning.

Wind whipped across the bleak countryside, and Luke drove slowly, concentrating on the road. It had continued to snow off and on last night, and the plows hadn't quite kept up. There were hazardous, icy spots everywhere.

Would he be able to take care of his father? He had instructions about the wound and the drain and the activity level, the recommended diet, what to watch out for. But the fact remained that he wasn't a trained medical professional, and his father was anything but a model patient.

"I can do it myself," Dad said the minute they pulled up in front of the house. He opened the car door.

"Wait," Luke said sharply. He turned off the car and hurried around to the passenger side as Dad tried, without success, to heave himself out of the car, cursing in obvious pain.

Luke grabbed for his father's flailing hands. "You're going to rip open your incision. Sit still a minute!"

"We, um, we'll just leave this on the porch." The voice behind Luke belonged to Hannah's mom, and he turned his head to see that, oh, great, Hannah was there, too. Both of them held dishes. They'd been kind and brought food.

"Thanks," he said distractedly as Dad made another effort to heave himself up. "We... Thanks."

There was a little clank as they set down their dishes, and the two of them picked up their cooler and headed off to the little path between their houses.

"Interfering women," Dad grunted, plenty loud enough for them to hear. His face was red, whether from exertion or embarrassment, Luke couldn't tell. Probably both.

"Look, you'll be faster if you let me help you. Swing your legs around first."

His father tried to do it, failed and swore as Luke reached down to help him move his legs. Luke tried to ignore the string of critical words as he used both hands to help his father stand. Then he supported him, gripping one ropey bicep and putting the other arm around his father. "Come on, let's get you inside. I set up a bed downstairs."

As they made their slow way toward the house, Luke couldn't help thinking about Hannah. Her uncomfortable expression just now. She wasn't used to the harsh conversations Luke and his father had on a regular basis.

Working with her yesterday, and then those

moments holding and kissing her…he'd never felt anything like it before. It had been perfect. A taste of the kind of love he'd never known he craved.

Of course, she'd skittered away as soon as the roads were clear, just as she'd skittered away now.

He looked at the crumbling concrete steps now adorned with fragrant, covered dishes. He listened to his father's complaints and foul language.

It wasn't going to happen with Hannah. Oh, she'd liked the kissing; he was experienced enough to know that. But it wouldn't amount to anything, not when she was from a good family and he was from a bad one.

Inside, he got his father to the bed just before he collapsed, his eyes closing. Luke knew he should get Dad to eat something, to drink the fluids he needed, but he couldn't bring himself to make the man stay awake when he was so clearly exhausted.

So he pulled off Dad's boots—something he'd done fairly often before, when Dad was drunk—and pulled the covers over his frail-looking form. He drew in a breath and let it out again, slowly.

Looking at his father twisted twin strands of love and exasperation around his heart. Dad was difficult, angry and often mean. But he was also tough and funny. And he needed help.

Dad would wake up and be mad about the way the room looked, devoid of the usual clutter and, instead, decorated for Christmas. He'd hate having to be cared for.

At the same time, it was obvious that Dad couldn't have managed all this alone. He was grateful to the old acquaintance from the hospital who'd called Luke and let him know his father was struggling and needed surgery.

Clearly, it was Luke's obligation, as a son and a Christian, to be here and help his father through this difficult time. He'd committed to it, and he'd do it.

Aside from workdays when the home healthcare person would come to be with, or at least visit, Dad, it would be all Luke, all the time, at least for these next couple of weeks.

The one benefit was that it would mean he couldn't spend any time with Hannah outside of work. That might mean he wouldn't have to push her away.

Despair rose in him as he thought about being here alone with his father, and then leaving Bethlehem Springs once Dad was on his feet. Especially as he contemplated never growing the thing that had sprung to life with Hannah during that fortuitous power outage in the barn.

He walked out and got Dad's bag, picked up the casseroles and brought them inside.

Why had God given him that taste of sweetness that was kissing Hannah, only to send him crashing back down to earth?

Or was Luke blaming God for his own mistakes?

Chapter Eleven

On Sunday night, Hannah waved goodbye to the nursing-home residents and climbed back into the car with Gabby, Sam and Sheniqua. The caroling had gone well and the others were obviously feeling festive, as they talked and laughed.

The air was crisp, the sky speckled with stars. Normally, Hannah would have loved the time with her cousin and friends, enjoyed singing her favorite Christmas songs. Now, though, she was in an ongoing state of confusion that kept her from focusing on the moment. What had that kiss meant, Friday night?

She hadn't seen Luke over the weekend, except for that awkward moment of bringing food over for him and his dad. She hadn't even wanted to come, but when Mom had struggled with the big cooler of food, of course, Hannah had to help. They'd meant to leave it on the porch for Luke and his dad to find when he got home, but when they'd arrived, Luke's car was already in the driveway. She and Mom had opened the cooler, gotten out the casseroles and put them on the porch while Luke struggled to get his father out of the car. When they'd realized that no one was in the mood for small talk, they'd quickly left.

Even though Hannah knew that nothing could come of their relationship, the way they'd held each other Friday night had taken her feelings to a deeper level. She'd felt her insides wrench when she'd seen he was having trouble getting his dad to accept help. She'd even wished she was his girlfriend, so that she'd have a legitimate right to help him.

When the other car pool of twentysomethings from church pulled up beside them, Hannah shook off her thoughts. She needed to be present with her friends, not pining after something that could never happen with Luke.

The other driver gestured for Gabby, who was driving, to open her window.

"We're going to go sing at the Hutchensons' place before we go home," he said. "Why don't you follow us?"

"Great idea!" exclaimed Gabby.

No, it wasn't; it was a terrible idea. "Luke's dad is probably resting," Hannah protested from the back seat. "I don't think we should disturb him."

"If the house is dark, we'll leave," Gabby promised. "But the poor man just got home from the hospital, and Luke's been taking care of him alone all weekend. I'm sure they could use some cheering up."

That might be true, but although both her imagination and a feeling of longing were strong, reality was another matter. Hannah didn't want to be the person cheering up Luke, because he didn't want her to be. He'd sent a text thanking her and her mother for the food, but it had been terse and impersonal.

"I just don't want to intrude," she said weakly, knowing she'd be overruled.

"We'll be right behind you," Gabby called to the other car, and they headed out across the dark, snowy landscape.

Thoughts of the closeness she'd shared with Luke pushed their way into Hannah's mind even as she tried to forget the comfort of his arms, the warmth in his eyes. That evening at the barn had been one of the best of her life.

But Luke had backed off. Possible reasons why nagged at her. She'd been a bad kisser. He'd done it out of pity. He didn't want to be involved. He'd thought better of it.

Even if he *had* wanted to pursue things, she

couldn't have done it because of her promise to keep Marnie's secret.

She was well and truly stuck.

"Why are you so quiet?" Sheniqua, beside her in the back seat, asked in a low tone. "Do you really not want to go? Is something wrong?"

"I'm fine," she said. Because she couldn't explain the truth to her friends, either, or her mom. She'd never kept a secret like this before, so she hadn't realized just how lonely it could be.

Following the other car, Gabby turned into Luke's driveway and pulled up halfway. "Lights are still on," she said. "Let's go."

A mixture of anticipation and dread put lead into Hannah's feet, and she was the last one out of the car. Goldie barked wildly, but from inside the house, Hannah noted. The dog trainer in her was glad that Luke and his father were keeping the dog inside.

There was a scolding command and then Goldie's barking stopped.

"'Hark! The Herald,' then 'Good King Wenceslas,'" Samantha suggested.

"That's so long, though." Hannah was hoping that by the time Luke and his father realized what was happening, she and the other carolers would be on their way out.

"It's a great story, though. Come on, cheer up." Gabby put an arm around Hannah. "What's got you so negative all of a sudden? You love caroling." Then she looked from Hannah to Luke's father's house, and the light dawned. "Ohhh. Did something happen with Luke? I heard you got stuck at Rescue Haven for a while Friday night…"

Great, now it was obvious to everyone. "Nothing. No. It's fine." She pasted a smile on her face, fluffed her hair and wished she'd worn something prettier than a parka and baggy jeans.

As they sang, she tried to focus on the words, the mediocre-to-good-to-great voices of her friends, the chilly, damp air. Anything but the man inside the house who'd rocked her world, her whole life.

But it was to no avail. Being close to Luke, caring more and more about him, learning his ways and his history—all of it filled her heart with unfamiliar longings that could never come to pass.

The curtain at the front window twitched, then opened. There was Luke, adjusting his father against pillows. The older man was frowning and waving a hand, like he didn't want to be there.

Hannah stopped singing and lifted a hand. "We should—" Then she noticed Luke's face and snapped her mouth closed.

Luke looked older than she'd ever seen him,

with lines on his forehead and bags under his eyes. His face held a thick stubble, much thicker than Friday night; it looked like he hadn't shaved since then.

He was doing yeoman's service taking care of his cantankerous father. And at least he, apparently, wanted to hear the music, because he moved to open the window slightly.

Everyone waved to the pair and they went on singing, adding a spontaneous extra round of "Angels We Have Heard on High." Luke's father stopped protesting and just watched. When they ended, Luke applauded, and after an encouraging word from Luke, his father did, too.

Luke held up a finger. "Hang on a minute, I'll come out." He closed the window and the curtains.

"I think they liked it!" Gabby was smiling.

Sheniqua put an arm around Hannah. "See, that wasn't so bad."

"You're right. I'm glad we came."

And then Luke opened the door and she wasn't so sure.

He walked out onto the porch in his bare feet, and they all clustered around and scolded him for that, and asked him how things were going, what he needed. He confessed he'd had a rough few days. He answered their questions about his father's health and state of mind with a wry half smile that said it all: his father was healing, but wasn't making Luke's caregiving easy.

Hannah stayed to the back of the crowd, half wishing he would notice her, half hoping he wouldn't.

And then he did, and he looked at her with such a strange mix of feelings in his face that Hannah felt overwhelmed with confusion. She hated herself for wanting him to care for her.

She couldn't stand to wait and see more about how he felt.

There was a solution. She slipped back to the edge of the crowd and grabbed Sheniqua's arm. "Look, I'm gonna run home," she said. "It's just next door."

"But it's dark…"

"I'm fine," Hannah said. Yes, she was a coward, but sometimes the coward's way was the best one.

Monday morning, Luke squealed into Rescue Haven's gravel drive at 9:37 a.m. and rushed into the barn. "Sorry I'm late," he called, and then realized that Hannah couldn't hear him.

She was vacuuming the floor and just waved and kept working. She was definitely acting weird after their kiss Friday night, and he should probably address it with her. But she seemed so focused. And then he realized that this was the day the benefactors were coming to check on their progress. Great, just great.

He grabbed a pail and rag and started washing windows. The sun was out today, and the whole place would look better with sun coming in…which it couldn't, given how dirty the windows were.

Once she turned off the vacuum to move some boxes, he called over to her. "Sorry I was late," he said. "The home nurse got there on time, but Dad was being a pill and I didn't want to leave until he'd settled down."

"How's he doing?" she asked, walking a few steps toward him.

He shook his head. "Physically, he's healing pretty well. Mentally…" He spread his hands. "He hates being laid up. He wants a drink. It's a struggle." He paused, then added, "I didn't get the chance to thank you for the caroling last night." *Because you took off like a herd of wolves was chasing you.*

"Sure." Suddenly she was back to being shy and embarrassed. She turned on the loud industrial vacuum cleaner abruptly and was off cleaning again.

An hour later, the place was sparkling, and while they still had a whole section of the barn to refloor and shelving to build, their progress was obvious. It was also obvious that they needed to talk—about the project and maybe about other stuff, as well. He sat on the bench and patted the seat beside him, and she sat down…as far away as possible.

She had to be thinking of that kiss, just as he was. But he was the older, more worldly one. He should take the bull by the horns.

"Look, we have to work together," he said. "That kiss shouldn't have happened."

"I know." She sounded miserable and she wouldn't look at him. "I'm sorry I led you on."

He stared at her bent head. "You didn't lead me on."

She didn't seem to hear him. She just stared at her knees.

He wanted to reach out and hold her. That was what he wanted every time he saw her now, and it was what couldn't happen. But he couldn't let her misperception go unremarked. "Hey," he said. "What's wrong? Where are you going in your head?"

She looked at him, her eyes filled with a kind of pain he hadn't known she had in her life.

"Where's this coming from? What happened?"

"It's nothing." She waved a hand. Her eyes were teary, making her denial totally unconvincing.

"Tell me." He moved to sit on the floor in front of her.

"Oh… I probably made too big a deal of it."

He waited.

She sucked in a breath and let it out shakily. "Marnie had this boyfriend," she said. "Maybe you knew him. Jack Anderson?"

Luke shook his head. "Doesn't sound familiar."

"Well, it's just as well. He was a jerk." She frowned. "He came upon me in the garage one day and, well…" She looked off across the barn. "He put his hands all over me."

"That's outrageous!" Indignation swelled in him. "You were how old?"

"Twelve," she said. "It was terrible of him, but I shouldn't have dressed the way I did."

He reeled back. "Are you joking? Why would you blame his actions on how you were dressed?"

She shrugged. "He told me that was why he did it. My shorts were too short. My shirt was too tight. He couldn't help it."

"No." Luke stood and paced a few steps away, then back again. "You were a child. I'm sure you didn't even know what being provocative meant."

"I didn't," she said. "But I did wear Marnie's and Samantha's hand-me-downs a lot, and some of them were probably too small. It's just…it's made me cautious. Around men."

He stifled the growl that wanted to come out

as he thought back. Hannah had been a cute, lively child, but he'd gone into the army before she got into her teens. Even when he'd been home on leave, he hadn't seen much of her. "Did you tell anyone?"

"I told Marnie. She said not to bother Mom with it, that guys are just like that. She agreed with him that if I dressed that way, I was asking for it."

"She was wrong." He knelt in front of her. "Do you get that now? She was absolutely wrong."

Hannah shrugged. "I kind of know that. And I know she was mad that her boyfriend had gone after me. She broke up with him soon after."

"I would hope so." He wanted to take her into his arms. Wanted to comfort her physically, but that was the last thing she needed after a story like that.

He cast his mind back where her story had started. "If that's why you think you led me on, know that it's absolutely not true," he said. "No matter what you were wearing, I'd have no right to take any kind of advantage."

"Oh, you didn't. I was totally on board." Then she blushed. "I mean, I shouldn't have been, but I was."

He tamped down the elation brought on by what she'd said. He stuck out a hand. "Friends?" he asked.

"Friends," she agreed, her smile wide and open. She even gave him a quick hug.

He hugged her back. It was hard to let go.

And he realized that this, being friends with Hannah, was not going to be easy.

Chapter Twelve

Saturday was unseasonably warm for December, so Hannah and her mother decided it was the perfect day to take Christmas-card photos with the twins. Their purpose was twofold. Of course, they wanted to share holiday greetings and good wishes. But they also wanted to let acquaintances know what had happened and that Marnie's twins were settled down in Bethlehem Springs with family.

"I'll get them into their Christmas outfits and do their hair," Mom said. "You set up a pretty backdrop. Maybe against the big pine tree?"

"Sounds good. And thank you for not mentioning that I'm terrible with clothes and hair." Hannah grinned wryly at her mother.

"You don't try, that's all." Mom patted Hannah's shoulder. "And speaking of, you should put on that red wool sweater, and I'll wear mine. Jeans are good, but maybe try a touch of lipstick."

Hannah made a face. "Do I have to?"

"No. You're beautiful just as you are."

Hannah hugged her mother, ran upstairs for her sweater and headed outside.

Pale winter sun shone, and with no breeze, Hannah was fine in a sweater and jeans. She moved a pretty wooden bench from the front porch to the evergreen tree, then brought a couple of poinsettias from the living room to set on either side of the bench. She pulled over a wooden rocking horse and an old-fashioned Speedy-Rite sled for props. Then she took a moment to sit on the bench to enjoy the day's peace and quiet.

After the discussion she'd had with Luke, she felt lighter, freer. She'd never told anyone else about the incident with Marnie's boyfriend, but it had haunted her for years. The fact that he'd listened, that he didn't think it was her fault, took away the power she'd always given it.

She and Luke were working well together. The benefactors had had to put off their visit until next week, which had meant they could relax a little. Everyone from Rescue Haven thought Mr. Romano and Mrs. Markowski would be happy with the training area.

The back door opened and Addie toddled out,

followed by Mom, who was holding Emmy. The twins wore matching red-and-white dresses, with knitted red caps and tights and fuzzy boots. They looked so adorable that tears came to Hannah's eyes.

She hadn't thought it possible to love them more than she had when she'd brought them home, but as it turned out, hearts could grow and love could grow. Now, her whole chest swelled with care and concern for them. Were she and Mom doing a good enough job? How was the absence of their mother affecting them inside?

Thinking of Marnie brought on a whole other set of issues. If only Marnie had sought and found the help she needed. She might be here with them to celebrate the holiday season.

No, she wouldn't. She'd still be estranged, cold to Hannah and her mother, and angry.

Hannah's unresolved feelings about Marnie gnawed at her, but not for long. Addie rushed over, rapturous at the sight of the rocking horse, and tried to climb on. Hannah laughed and helped her, and then Emmy wanted to try it out.

"We'd better get these shots taken before they get messed up. It's kind of muddy out here." Mom wiped a smear off Addie's boot and adjusted Emmy's hat. "Girls, sit on the bench and smile."

Emmy climbed up. Addie's forehead wrinkled and she opened her mouth. A "no" was clearly forthcoming.

"After we take some pretty pictures of pretty girls, we'll share a cookie!" Mom pulled a crumbled sandwich cookie out of her pocket and winked at Hannah.

"Cookie. Okay." Addie quickly climbed up beside her sister. They smiled and laughed while Hannah snapped pictures with her phone and Mom adjusted dresses and hats.

"Now, we need to do a family photo," Hannah said as Mom delivered the promised cookie, breaking it in half for the twins.

Mom's chin wobbled and she didn't look at Hannah. When would that word—*family*—stop causing them pain? "I'll set up the camera and do the timer," Hannah said through a surprisingly tight throat.

Getting the angle right was tough. Hannah propped the phone on the arm of an Adirondack chair they'd never taken inside, but that was too low. By the time she'd run inside for a stack of books to raise it, the twins were losing focus. Setting the timer, rushing back into the picture herself and then trying to keep the twins smiling at the camera proved to be a losing proposition.

"You should call Luke," Mom said after a couple of failed efforts. "See if he'll run over and take it."

Hannah frowned. "I don't want to bother them." Did Mom think something was going on between Hannah and Luke? Was she trying to make something happen, matchmaking?

As if their words and thoughts had summoned them, Luke and his father appeared, walking slowly, side by side, from the path that connected their properties. Luke held his father's arm.

"Mercy, what are you doing out of the house?" Mom rushed toward the porch. "Let me get you a better chair."

Addie and Emmy sat together on the bench, studying the new arrivals. They stared wide-eyed at Luke's dad, walking so slowly and carefully, using a cane. Then Addie called out a bold "Hi!" and Mr. Hutchenson's face lit up with a smile, and when he said, "Hi, yourself, little lady," and made a face at Addie, both girls giggled.

It was apparent where Luke had gotten his ease with children.

"I hope you don't mind," Luke said as Mom came back with a chair. "We needed to get out, and we needed a destination. It's a nice day."

As Luke and Mom helped Mr. Hutchenson to sit down, Hannah wondered what was behind Luke's words. Judging from the circles under his eyes, he'd had a sleepless night. But there was no hint of impatience in his expression or movements.

"Got stir-crazy," Mr. Hutchenson admitted. "Not used to lying around the house."

"You did the right thing," Mom declared, "and you're welcome to sit with us as long as you like. The twins will cheer anyone up."

Especially their grandfather.

Confusion crowded Hannah's mind. Mr. Hutchenson wasn't well. Didn't he deserve to know his granddaughters? To know that these adorable girls *were* his granddaughters?

At the same time, he was only sitting and making nice because he was sick. Normally, he'd be staying out late, closing the bars and causing trouble. In full health, he wasn't the right influence for the twins, and Marnie had known that.

"We need help with our Christmas-card photos," Mom said. "Can you take a few for us?"

"Sure thing." Luke took the camera while Hannah and Mom each sat a twin in their lap.

Again, Hannah felt a pang. Truth be known, Luke and his father were part of this family.

The photography session still wasn't easy—getting all four of them to smile naturally at the same time wasn't a walk in the park—but with Luke laughing and encouraging them, it turned from a chore into fun. Luke teased and cajoled the twins and they clearly responded to him.

"They haven't had much of a male influence, I don't think," Mom said as they posed the twins on the sleigh. "They seem to really blossom with it."

The weight on Hannah's shoulders got heavier. She'd said she'd try to find a man to bring into their lives…but her project of dating had stopped before it had even gotten started. She'd just been too busy. Way too busy to look around and meet potential partners.

She didn't want to examine the other reason that hadn't been a priority.

If she wasn't going to date, there was another way for the girls to have a male influence: telling the truth. Letting Luke and his father know that they were related to the girls.

Emmy let out a terrific sneeze, and Hannah hurried to wipe her nose.

"Bobby used to sneeze just like that, loud," Luke's father said.

Hannah froze.

Mom misinterpreted the expression on Hannah's face. "Don't worry about a little sneezing," she said. "Kids always do that. It doesn't mean she's sick."

"Ain't that the truth," agreed Mr. Hutchenson.

"Speaking of Bobby, Luke's promised to take me to see him next week."

Hannah felt a chill unrelated to the cloud that passed over the sun.

Keeping the secret Marnie had charged her with might not be in her hands. What if Mr. Hutchenson, or Luke, guessed the truth about the twins?

Monday morning, Luke sensed a cooling in Hannah's attitude toward him. Man, did this woman ever run hot and cold! She'd seemed so friendly when he and his father had helped with the photography session on Saturday... At least, she'd seemed friendly at first. What had changed?

Bobby. Again, with the mention of his incarcerated brother, Hannah had gone cold.

It didn't seem very Christian of her, and moreover, it didn't seem like Hannah. She'd been friends with some of the outcast kids in her elementary school, from what he could remember. She didn't speak disparagingly about her cousin Samantha's struggle with alcoholism, something Corbin and Samantha had told Luke about when they'd been helping to clean up after Thanksgiving dinner.

Hannah was an all-around good, accepting person.

So what was it about Bobby?

Or maybe it was something about Luke himself.

They had no time to work anything out, though, because Reese came in and told them that Mrs. Markowski and Mr. Romano were coming on Thursday and expected the project to be near completion. They'd made good progress, but they weren't far enough along, so they focused and worked all morning. The place got to be a mess again, with paint and cleaning products and flooring materials everywhere, but it was all part of the process.

Luke was just starting to think they would get it done when Hannah got a call that made her frown.

"What's wrong?" he asked.

"Emmy's sick," she said, biting her lip. "She's over at the Learn-and-Play, and they want me to come get her. She has a fever."

"Hey, it happens." He remembered when Nicolette had gotten sick, which had happened pretty frequently. "It's probably nothing, but you might want to take her to the pediatrician just to be sure."

Hannah grabbed her coat and pawed through her purse. "Where are my keys? I need to get over there. I could hear her crying when Gabby called."

"They're right here." Luke picked up her keys

from the hook beside the coatrack. "Come on. I'll go over with you."

"Thank you!" She looked relieved, and he almost thought she was going to cling to his arm as they walked across Rescue Haven's big lawn and gravel road.

The Learn-and-Play was furnished with small chairs around a couple of tables, a row of high chairs along a taller table, colorful rugs and bins of toys. Luke swallowed hard, remembering when Nicolette had gone to a day care similarly decorated. Maybe they were all this way. He'd often been the one to pick her up after work, and she'd always gotten so excited to see him, running to him, holding her arms up, calling him Da-da.

Then he heard Emmy's wail, coming from the row of cribs along one wall.

"She feels warm, and her temperature seems to be rising," Gabby told them. "I put her over in the cubby nook in a crib, just to keep her away from the other kids, but she doesn't like being separated from Addie. It's probably inevitable that Addie will catch whatever she has, too, but right now she's fine."

Hannah hurried over to Emmy and picked her up. "She's burning up. I need to take her to the doctor, but what about Addie? Mom's alone at the bakery today, and—"

Gabby waved a hand. "Don't give it another thought. I'll drive Addie over to your house at the end of the day. You and Emmy will probably be home by then, but if you're not, your Mom will be, right?"

"Yes." But Hannah still looked worried. "How can I just stick Emmy in her car seat, crying like this?"

Luke held out his hand. "Give me your keys. I'll drive while you sit in the back with her. You can call the doctor's office, too, let them know we're coming." He walked over to the bins, found the one labeled *Emmy* and pulled out her little bag. From the labeled hook, he grabbed Emmy's coat.

Hannah's shoulders relaxed. "You'd do that for me? That would be such a huge help." She took the coat from him and eased it onto the crying child.

They left the Learn-and-Play and carried Emmy and her things through cold, blowing snow to Hannah's car. Luke hurried to open the back door, then scooped Emmy out of Hannah's arms and plunked her into the car seat. Her hair was damp with sweat, and he didn't want her to get a chill on top of everything else. "Get in beside her," he told Hannah as he tossed the diaper bag onto the passenger seat and slid behind the wheel. "Call the pediatrician, then GPS the address for me. It's the one out on Todd Farm Road, right? But I don't know the fastest way to get there."

As Hannah followed his instructions, patting Emmy the whole time, the baby's cries downgraded into whimpers, and Luke felt something he hadn't felt in a long time: a sense of rightness. He was where he needed and wanted to be, where God intended him to be.

Wouldn't it be nice if he could have that feeling all the time?

Chapter Thirteen

Inside the pediatrician's office, Hannah hurried to the receptionist's desk, carrying Emmy, Luke behind her. "I'm Hannah Antonicelli and this is Emmy. I called?"

"Right, have a seat." The receptionist gave Luke a speculative glance, obvious enough for Hannah to notice even amid her worry.

Luke was an attention-getter, all right. Especially as he scooped Emmy from her arms so that Hannah could fill out the paperwork and walked around the office, cooing and bouncing her gently, settling her fussing.

A man that handsome who was also a baby whisperer? No wonder the receptionist was staring.

Hannah sat down and filled out the papers, dug in her purse for the brand-new insurance card, thankful the visit would be covered. It was only their second time in the office; on their first, they hadn't had it all straightened out yet and had had to pay the full cost of the appointment.

The pretty receptionist got up and walked over to Luke, then tickled Emmy's chin, rousing Hannah's ire. Was it really protocol for her to flirt so obviously with the man of the family?

Although maybe she'd looked at Emmy's chart and seen that there was only a mother and grandmother listed, no father. And maybe she wasn't really flirting. Maybe Hannah was being oversensitive.

Whatever the reason, Hannah's insecurities kicked in. Unlike the neat, scrubs-clad receptionist, Hannah was dirty from work, her jeans old and faded, her plaid shirt out of style. She reached up to straighten her hair and found a piece of straw from the barn in it. She was a hayseed, no mistake about that.

The door to the back office opened. "Hannah Antonicelli?" called a white-clad nurse.

Hannah took Emmy from Luke and handed the clipboard to the receptionist, then headed toward the open door.

"Dad can come, too," the nurse said.

Hannah glanced back to see Luke raising an eyebrow at her. *Your call*, he seemed to be saying.

She wanted him with her. And her jealous,

insecure side didn't want to leave him out there with the flirty receptionist. She gave him a nod, and he followed her back to the office.

The nurse had barely finished the preliminaries before the doctor came in and took over. "What's going on with this sweetheart?" she asked. She glanced at the computer where the nurse had entered Emmy's basics, then had Hannah hold her while she listened to her chest and felt her forehead.

Hannah started to relax a little. This was why she'd liked Dr. Marcy on their first visit: she was hands on and seemed to take her time, and obviously, she had a way with babies.

"We're going to give her something for her fever right now, and some for you to take home for later. It sounds like she's got the same little flu that's been going around. Happens every year, and most likely, everyone in her day care will get it. Including her twin, and possibly you." She nodded at Hannah and Luke. Then she frowned. "Are you Dad? I thought…" She leaned toward the computer.

"No," Luke said. "I'm a friend of the family."

"Okay to talk in front of him?" the doctor asked Hannah.

A cold claw of fear reached into Hannah's chest. There were things Luke shouldn't know, and she'd only now realized they could come out in this visit.

"Sure," she said faintly. Because, of course, Emmy's health was the priority.

The doctor administered the medicine and gestured Hannah toward a chair. "Go ahead, sit and hold her. She's uncomfortable with the fever, but it's clear that she's bonded to you."

As if in agreement, Emmy settled into Hannah's chest, thumb in her mouth.

The doctor studied the chart again and then turned on her wheeled stool and faced Hannah. "Did you get the chance to do that parent questionnaire on development?"

Hannah groaned softly. "I completely forgot."

"Do it soon," the doctor said.

There was something in her tone. "Should I be worried?"

The doctor rolled her chair closer and held a pencil toward Emmy, who grasped it, then dropped it. "How many words can she say?"

Hannah frowned. "She says 'Mama' and 'ball' and 'Gamma.' She calls me 'Hah' sometimes and 'Mama' sometimes."

"She says 'pizza,'" Luke contributed, lightening the atmosphere a little.

The doctor smiled. "That's good then. Does she put words together yet?"

"No. Addie, her twin, does, but Emmy doesn't."

"Very common in twins," the doctor said. "One will be a little delayed in speech and the other takes over the talking." She squeaked a colorful stuffed octopus in front of Emmy and then held it out to her.

Emmy reached for it, then dropped it.

"Is that normal?" both Luke and Hannah asked at the same time.

"It seems like she has a couple of delays," the doctor said. "That's common, and she might catch up quickly on her own. A lot of kids do. But early intervention has really good outcomes, and it's a free service from the State of Ohio."

Hannah swallowed. "You think she needs early intervention? Is there something we—or her mom—could have done differently to prevent this?"

"It's doubtful," the pediatrician said cheerfully. "Mostly, delays like this are genetic. I remember your mom said you and your sister were early walkers and talkers, so it's not coming from your side. You might want to check into Dad's history, if it's available. But regardless, filling out the questionnaire is the first step of early intervention paperwork, and I think it's worth doing."

"Of course, I will." Hannah's stomach churned as they gathered Emmy's things and walked out of the office, slowly, because Emmy had fallen asleep on Hannah's shoulder. Luke carried everything and opened doors, then helped to get Emmy into her car seat.

She loved having his help. Not so much the physical, although that was great, but the emotional. Having someone there to talk over what the doctor had said and figure out what to do next.

Of course, Hannah was blessed to have her mother, who would be eager to hear everything, who'd help Hannah complete the questionnaires on the twins, who was every bit an involved grandma, a live-in one. Lots of single moms didn't have that kind of support, and Hannah shouldn't be sad just because she didn't have a man.

She looked over at Luke's profile as he confidently, competently drove her little car back to her house, brushing aside her suggestion that they go get his car at Rescue Haven, assuring her that he'd get it tomorrow, that he could use his dad's vehicle in an emergency.

Why was he being so helpful and supportive? Did he care for her, at least a little, or was he just being kind?

And what would he think if he found out the truth, that he was the twins' uncle?

Wednesday morning, Luke and Hannah climbed out of Hannah's car at Rescue Haven.

Reese strode toward them immediately, looking agitated. "We have a problem," he said.

Luke tried to get his head in the game, but it was hard to do. He'd felt so close to Hannah after that doctor visit for Emmy, and the feeling still electrified the air between them.

Yesterday, even though Dad had developed some worrisome symptoms requiring an unexpected ER visit—one that had taken all day, although everything had turned out fine—Luke had felt an internal patience and contentment that was alien to him.

He cared for Hannah. He wanted to explore getting closer. That had become clearer and clearer to him, and it had crystalized in the pediatrician's office when he'd wanted nothing more than to be that dad the receptionist and then the doctor had thought him to be.

"What's going on?" Hannah asked Reese.

"They're here," Reese said. "Aunt Catherine and Mr. Romano."

"Now?" Luke stared toward the barn where, sure enough, a large, late-model SUV was parked. "I thought they were coming tomorrow."

"So did we," Reese said, "but when there's that much money involved, they get to change their plans at the last minute. Apparently, Aunt Catherine heard about a sale at one of her favorite department stores in Cleveland, tomorrow only, so they switched to today."

Luke looked at Hannah, who was looking back at him. "I hope you had the chance to clean things up from Monday," she said.

He stared at her. "I was out yesterday, with Dad," he said. "I thought you worked, though."

She shook her head slowly. "Mom couldn't take yesterday off," she said, "so I had to stay home with Emmy."

"I wish you two would have communicated with each other," Reese said. "Come on, let's go face the music."

Gabby came out of the Learn-and-Play. "I'll take Addie," she said, holding out her arms for the baby. "You guys need to get down to the barn and do damage control. Mrs. Markowski already called over here to find out why it's such a mess over there."

"Right." Luke swallowed as he thought about the way they'd left the barn on Monday. They'd been right in the middle of laying down the final section of new flooring when Hannah had gotten the call about Emmy, and they'd dropped everything and gone to her. If Hannah hadn't been in yesterday to fix things up...

They walked in the door to find Mr. Romano pacing around tools and paint cans and rolls of artificial turf left haphazardly on the floor. Mrs.

Markowski was on her phone, but she clicked off the call as soon as Hannah, Luke and Reese walked in.

"This isn't at all what we had in mind," she scolded.

"Very unprofessional," Romano chimed in. "I expected you to be much further along."

"It'll get done," Luke said firmly. "We've had a couple of family medical situations that have slowed us down, but it's under control now."

"You saw the plans," Hannah said, "and we're following them exactly. The last stages of a project like this are messy, but it's going to end up great."

Mrs. Markowski's eyes narrowed. "I hope you're right. I had my doubts about entrusting this to a Hutchenson, even in part. I hope there's been no cheating with the funds you've used so far."

Luke's insides exploded with shame and rage, and he opened his mouth to lay into the woman. Would've done it, too, except that Reese put a hand on his shoulder and Hannah touched his arm.

"There are receipts for everything," Hannah said to the older woman, her voice stiff.

"Luke's done stellar work for us ever since he started," Reese insisted.

As the conversation and the excuses and the

reassurances continued, Luke's emotions spiraled down.

He could never overcome his name in this town. He hadn't lived up to expectations.

He was a Hutchenson, through and through.

Finally, Reese walked the two elders to the door, talking to them in a soothing voice as they continued to complain.

Luke turned on Hannah and let out his frustration. "If you hadn't stayed home yesterday without telling me, this wouldn't have happened."

"You did the same thing," she snapped back. "How was I supposed to know your dad would need to go to the ER? At least you knew Emmy was sick."

They glared at each other.

Hannah's eyes practically sent out sparks, and her hair was rumpled where she'd clawed it back.

And she was right. He blew out a breath and unclenched his fists. "Sorry. You're right. It wasn't your fault."

She'd opened her mouth as if to continue the fight, but at his words, she went still, looking at his face.

Man, she was pretty.

"It's not your fault, either," she said finally. "But we do have to fix it. I need for this to get done, on time and to their specifications, and you do, too."

"Look, let's work all day and get the project back to where we're supposed to be," he said as Reese walked back toward them. "Then maybe tonight, we could go get dinner and figure out a plan to win them back."

She tilted her head, looking at him.

Suddenly he felt like he'd just asked her out on a date. His palms sweat as he waited for her response.

"I can't," she said finally. "It's a good idea, but I need to get home and relieve Mom. Emmy's better, but that means she's a handful, and Addie is, too."

"When it gets down to it, I shouldn't, either. I have to take care of Dad," he said.

"No, you don't." Reese planted his hands on his hips. "If you two think you can meet and figure something out tonight, do it. I'll go sit with your dad, and Gabby can help your mom with the twins."

"But what about Izzy? Gabby can't take her to where Emmy's been sick."

"That's the beauty of Nana," Reese said. "She doesn't get as much alone time with Izzy as she'd like. She'll be thrilled to have a whole evening with her."

"Thank you!" Spontaneously, Hannah hugged Reese and then Luke. It was just a friendly hug, but Luke felt it from head to toe, and in more than a friendly way. "I'm going to get to work," she said, and hurried over to the training area.

"Seize the day, man." Reese raised his eyebrows and punched Luke in the arm, lightly. "Take her somewhere nice."

Luke thought about it. "I just might."

"And get the job done," Reese added. "Rescue Haven, and a bunch of dogs and kids, need for this to work."

"Will do." Luke nodded, and then headed over to where Hannah was already working.

He'd throw himself into it today, and maybe by tonight, he'd be tired enough not to feel like his heart would explode at the thought of taking Hannah Antonicelli out to a nice dinner.

No matter that they'd be talking shop. This was going to be a date.

Chapter Fourteen

As they walked into Giannone's, an Italian restaurant on the edge of Cleveland, Hannah was glad she'd decided to wear a dress.

Partly because most of the other patrons were dressed up.

And partly because of the way Luke had looked at her when she'd come downstairs.

The faintest hint of a wolfish grin had flashed across his face, immediately replaced by a more gentlemanly, appreciative expression. "You look nice" was all he'd said, but she could tell he meant it.

He looked nice, too. More than nice. What was it about that jeans-and-a-sport-coat look that got to her? Not too fancy or too preppy, but dressed up enough to show he was making an effort.

Not to mention the way his jacket emphasized his broad shoulders...

"Well, Hannah Antonicelli!" The waitress who came to the hostess stand to help them was middle-aged, plump and slightly familiar. "I haven't seen you in a blue moon."

"Rosemary?" She hugged the woman, a distant relative, and then turned to include Luke in their little circle. "Rosemary, this is Luke Hutchenson. Luke, Rosemary Brody. She's my, what, second cousin once removed?"

"Yes, and my uncle owns this place. And you look like a Hutchenson," Rosemary said, shaking Luke's hand. "I knew your brother, Bobby, years ago."

At the mention of his name and his brother, Luke frowned, and Hannah's heart ached for him. It must be so hard to always be explaining that your brother was in prison, so nerve-racking to wonder what intrusive questions might need to be answered or dodged.

But Rosemary didn't ask more about Bobby. "It's good to meet you," she said, looking around the restaurant. "I'm going to seat you two by the fireplace, if that's all right. It's a cold night."

As they walked across the half-full restaurant, the smells of garlic and marinara and warm bread made Hannah's stomach growl. She breathed in the scent of home. Her father's side of the family had been fantastic cooks, and Hannah had grown up loving Italian food.

They sat down with menus, next to a warm fire, as if in a world of their own. Rosemary took their drink orders, and when they both ordered soda, she shook her head. "No wine?"

Simultaneously, Hannah and Luke shook their heads. "I don't drink," he said as she said, "No, thanks."

"Fine, fine." Rosemary went off to get their beverages, and Hannah thought: how many men are there who don't drink? He's so perfect for me!

Don't go there, she scolded herself. But it was hard not to, when her heart raced with joy just to be here, tonight, with Luke.

They placed their orders and were soon presented with salads and hot, fragrant Italian bread. Hannah was half-afraid Rosemary would sit down and join them—Hannah remembered her as a superfriendly talker—but after the initial flurry, she seemed to fade purposely into the background. Luke and Hannah dug in to the bread and salads.

After a few minutes, Hannah sat back. "If I'm going to eat my lasagna, I'd better slow down," she said.

"Not a bad idea. I understand portions are big here." He sat back, too, and gave her a half smile. "I know I told you before, but I want to apologize again for blaming you earlier today. None of that was your fault."

She waved a hand. "Same goes for me. I shouldn't have jumped on you, either. You had no choice but to take care of your dad. And Luke—" she touched his hand "—I'm sorry about what Mrs. Markowski said. That was an awful accusation about the funds, and a ridiculous one, too."

"Not entirely." He shook his head. "It did make me mad, but I thought about it later. Who knows what all Bobby did in this region when I was overseas? And Dad hasn't been the most law-abiding citizen, either. No wonder people question my integrity."

"You're not defined by your family," she said.

Rosemary appeared again to check on them. "When you dress up, you look just like your sister," she said over her shoulder as she walked away.

Hannah's breath caught. Did she look like Marnie, really?

"She's right, you know," Luke said.

"No, she's not. Marnie was the pretty one, not me."

"I disagree," he said lightly, obviously just to be nice.

She waved her hand. "It's fine. It didn't do Marnie any good to be pretty." To her shock, her eyes filled with tears.

"Hey," he said, reaching across the table to clasp her hand, "are you okay?"

She pulled away, sniffed and wiped at her eyes with a napkin. "I'm fine. I'm usually just mad at Marnie, but I guess somewhere in there, I'm sad, too."

"Of course you are." He gave her a minute to compose herself, taking a piece of bread, breaking it so that steam rose out in a visible cloud, spreading it with soft butter. He held it out to her, one eyebrow raised.

She laughed a little and shook her head. "In a minute. You eat it."

He set it down on his bread plate instead. Then he reached across the table, put a hand on her forearm and looked into her eyes. "You're pretty, too, Hannah. Inside and out."

"I…" She trailed off and their gazes tangled. The warmth from the fire, the fragrance of the bread and, most of all, the feeling of his gentle, callused hand on her arm… All of it stole her breath and made her wish for things she couldn't have.

There was a reason she couldn't have them, but right now, it was hard to remember what that reason was. Hard to think. Hard to do anything but look into Luke's eyes.

"Here you go," Rosemary sang. "Lasagna for you, and baked manicotti for him. Enjoy!"

The mood was broken, and that was a good thing. Hannah thanked Rosemary, and drew in a couple of calming breaths. She glanced over at Luke and it looked like he was doing the same thing.

They started in on their steaming food. Strands of cheese stretched from Hannah's lasagna to her fork, and with Luke, she felt fine about breaking the threads with her fingers. Luke took a giant bite of manicotti and closed his eyes.

When he opened them and smiled at her, the corners of his eyes crinkled. "This is joyous food. I'm glad we came."

"Me, too." He was so fun and appealing. It was hard to look away.

Stop. Get to work. She nodded, wiped her mouth and cleared her throat. "We need to figure out how to fix what went wrong at work today," she said.

Did his face fall a little bit? Why? Did he *want* this to be purely a social dinner?

But it couldn't be that, no matter what Luke wanted, and it was best to be up front about it, for his sake and for hers, too. "We have to regain their confidence and impress them."

"Right." He sighed.

"I know it's not going to be easy. Mrs. Markowski was awful toward you."

He lifted his hands, palms up. "She's not entirely wrong about my family. And you, especially, need this job to go to full-time, for the twins' sake. Right?"

"Right." His wording made her curious. "Do *you* want your job to go full-time, too?"

"Maybe."

It wasn't the answer she'd been hoping to hear, and she realized that she really, really wanted Luke to stay around for the long haul. It was hard to imagine her life without him somewhere in it.

"I was thinking," he said. "Doesn't Mrs. Markowski have a little dog?"

"Oh, my, yes. Pinky is notorious." Hannah had offered to train the little creature, but it had never worked out.

"Okay, look. Mrs. Markowski strikes me as the powerhouse of the pair. Romano talks big, but seems to me he'll do whatever Mrs. Markowski says."

"He will," she said slowly. "What do you have in mind?"

"If we can get the training area up and running, would you be able to get Pinky to do something in it? Some kind of agility work or tricks?"

She frowned. "I might, but it wouldn't be a sure thing. The dog doesn't respond real well to anyone but her."

"Even better," he said. "We'll get everything set up nicely, and then get her to come over and bring Pinky, and you can teach her to teach the dog to, I don't know, jump over a hurdle or go through a tunnel or something. I mean, if you can get me to do tricks with Goldie, you can get Mrs. Markowski to work with her dog."

Hannah tilted her head to one side, thinking. "And if she's invested, she'll buy in."

"I think she'd like to have a role. She could even demonstrate it to other people, and talk up the training that can be done there."

"I'd have to get her to wear casual clothes," she said doubtfully.

"Why? If she likes wearing dresses and suits...isn't that what they wear at those dog shows on TV, anyway?"

That made Hannah snort, and then she thought about it. "You know, she'd love to be able to participate in dog shows. Pinky is the center of her universe, now that her daughter's away at the university."

"So what are our steps?" He pushed his plate away. "I think we can get the place cleaned up and workable tomorrow."

"And then tomorrow evening, we can meet and make a training plan to present to her. Or... I could do that alone, I guess. I can't ask Mom, or Gabby, to take care of the twins every night."

"And I have to be nearby for Dad. But we can combine forces at one of our houses, maybe. I could come over, or you could bring the twins to our place. I don't want to dump this problem on you."

She opened her mouth to say that wasn't necessary, but shut it again. It *wasn't* necessary, not strictly, but she'd get better ideas if Luke was working at her side.

And more than that, she *wanted* him to be there.

While they'd been talking, Rosemary had unobtrusively cleared their plates, and now she came to the table with the check.

Luke took it from her and pulled out his wallet. When Hannah went for her purse, he waved a hand at her. "I've got this."

"But—"

"Let him pay," Rosemary advised. "You two are so cute. Just like Bobby and Marnie used to be, when they came here."

For a minute, Hannah didn't take in her words. Then Luke paused in the midst of pulling out a credit card. "Bobby and Marnie used to come here?"

"Yes, they did."

Hannah felt her face go hot while the rest of her body turned to ice.

"Huh," he said, and handed Rosemary the card. "Here you go. Dinner was great."

"It was," Hannah choked out.

She went through the motions of finishing

their plans for tomorrow, saying goodbye to Rosemary, putting on her coat. As Luke ushered her outside, she felt like she'd dodged a bullet...but one that was going to come back for her, again and again.

She was going to have to tell Luke the truth. He needed to hear it from her before he figured it out himself.

She'd do it as soon as they worked through this crisis with the benefactors.

The next evening, after dinner, Luke came over as they'd discussed. To Hannah's surprise, though, his father was at his side. The older man was walking more upright. His color was good, and he wasn't holding Luke's arm.

"You look so much better!" Hannah's mother hurried to take the two men's coats. "Are you sure you want to be around the twins, though? Emmy's better, and Addie doesn't seem to have caught her cold, but—"

"I wanted to see them," the older man said simply. He sat down in the chair Mom indicated and studied the girls. Addie was having her usual after-dinner spurt of energy, running through the house. Emmy had reverted to crawling, as she sometimes did when she was tired. She moved closer to the older man and pulled herself up on his leg, making him smile.

"I should have cleared it with you," Luke said, "but I figured that since Dad's feeling better, we might as well put him to work helping to baby-sit the twins."

"Glad to do it," Mr. Hutchenson said.

"And I'm glad for the help. Now, you two go sit at the kitchen table," Mom ordered. "Get your work done. We'll handle the girls."

"But I feel bad you're always having to do that," Hannah protested.

"They're my granddaughters," Mom said. "Why wouldn't I take care of them as much as I can?"

"Makes sense," Mr. Hutchenson said. "Wish I had grandchildren."

Mr. Hutchenson's words reverberated in Hannah's mind. He'd wanted to see the girls. He wished he had grandkids.

Luke's father actually *had* grandchildren and was even now bending down to help build a block tower with one of them.

Keeping the relationship a secret seemed more wrong than ever.

She tried to focus on making a training plan with Luke, but she kept straining to hear the conversation between her mom and Mr. Hutchenson in the other room, which resulted in her making mistake after mistake. Computer work had never been her strong suit, anyway, and she was a two-finger typist. Luke laughed at her, and eventually, he took over at the computer. Once they'd figured out a plan and made it look nice, they emailed Mrs. Markowski with their proposal.

But as Luke and his father left, she saw the older man studying Emmy and Addie thoughtfully. It almost seemed like he knew something.

She was going to have to break her promise to Marnie. She had to tell Luke—tell both of them—and the sooner the better.

On Saturday, just before Luke and his father started the complicated check-in procedures for visiting Bobby at the prison, he turned to his father. "You sure you're up for this?"

Dad's hand went reflexively to his incision site, but he nodded his head. "I have to do it."

That was how he'd been talking for the last couple of days, and it was concerning to Luke. As he submitted to the search and produced his ID, then explained the reasons for their visit and their relationship to the incarcerated man, Luke worried.

Had the most recent doctor's visit, which Luke hadn't been able to attend because of work, let Dad know something serious about his health, something he wasn't telling Luke? "Is there some reason for the urgency?" he asked as they waited to be cleared.

"Yes, there's a reason!" Dad glared at him. "I'm old and I'm sick and life's short." Then his face softened. "You're too young to understand. I'm going to pull through this recovery, but lying in that hospital made me think. I don't want to have regrets, that's all."

"Makes sense." If they'd been a different kind of father and son, he'd have hugged the man, but they weren't.

As they walked to the visiting area, the armed guards and clanking double doors jolted Luke. How had Bobby let himself get to this place? Of course, he deserved to be here, given that he'd contributed to a man's death, but still, the thought that his little brother lived in this environment turned his stomach.

He should have been there for Bobby. Maybe there was something he could have done.

Bobby came through the door, wearing the orange jumpsuit Luke had only ever seen on television, and Luke's heart twisted as he stared at his brother. Bobby was clean-shaven, but his face was leaner than the last time Luke had seen him, his eyes more serious. He'd always been easygoing and fun, but now, he didn't smile; he lifted his jaw like he wanted to prove his toughness.

The guard checked their hands before permitting a handshake. It wasn't a maximum-security prison, but the next level down, and the precautions made sense.

After a few forced pleasantries had faded into silence, Luke plunged in. "Look, Bobby. I'm sorry I wasn't around to help you kind of navigate life. I didn't know my responsibility then. But I've changed, and I realize I let you down."

Bobby studied him steadily. "What made you change?"

Talking about the deep things in life was uncomfortable, and Luke was bad at it, but he handed over the bible he'd gotten permission to bring in. "Reading this. I hope you'll read it, too."

Bobby's face broke into a smile, the first of the visit. "I already have."

Luke couldn't believe it. "You've...found faith?"

Dad snorted.

"I'm a work in progress, but I'm trying," Bobby said. "I'll take the bible, if you don't mind, and share it with someone who needs it. Thanks." He put his hand on the leather-bound New Testament, almost with reverence. "As far as letting me down...seems to me I'm the one who let you two down. It was my responsibility to be a good citizen, and I didn't live up to it. I'm sorry."

Luke's throat tightened as he heard his brother

take full blame for what he'd done. Prison had finally made Bobby grow up.

Dad cleared his throat. "If I can get a word in edgewise, with you church types…"

One corner of Bobby's mouth turned up and he exchanged a glance with Luke before turning to Dad. "You doing okay? With the surgery and all?"

Luke was surprised Bobby had paid attention to the letter he'd written about Dad's situation. In the past, that would have gone right over his self-absorbed head, but it seemed Bobby really was changing.

Dad waved a hand. "Fine, fine." He paused, then added, "I guess you heard about Marnie Antonicelli?"

"Yeah. Sad thing." He shook his head, two lines appearing between his eyebrows. "Great girl."

"When exactly were you two together?" Dad asked, leaning forward. It was a strange question. Luke had known Bobby and Marnie had dated, but he hadn't thought it was anything serious.

He had a sudden flash of memory: that restaurant, Hannah's cousin, her comment that Hannah and Luke reminded her of Bobby and Marnie.

Bobby looked off into the rest of the noisy room, frowning. "I had a couple real nice months with her, right before I got in here. We might have made something of it, if I hadn't been such a fool."

"Did she stay in touch?" Dad probed.

"Nah. Didn't want anything to do with a felon." He lifted his hands, palms up. "Which I understand."

"Then you might not know," Dad said, "that she had twins."

"That she had…" Bobby stared at Dad. "When?"

It hit Luke like a bucket of cold water to the face, what Dad was getting at, but it was a ridiculous notion. "Those girls can't be his."

Dad didn't answer. He just watched Bobby.

"Actually…" Bobby stared at Dad. A drop of sweat rolled down his face. "Do you know… How old are they?"

"The math works out," Dad said quietly.

"What?" Luke's world reeled. If Addie and Emmy were Bobby's daughters, then that meant Luke was their uncle. It meant Dad was their grandfather.

He felt breathless, like he'd just been running hard. "What made you think of this?" he asked his father.

"It was when you said Emmy was behind in walking and talking," Dad said. "Bobby was slow to walk and talk. She has the same sneeze, too. And then when I got to studying those girls, I could see the similarities."

As his father and brother talked haltingly through the angles, as Dad showed a picture he'd sneaked on his phone, Luke's mind spun. How was he going to tell Hannah?

There was no way she already knew. If she'd suspected, she'd have told him. Told Dad. Wouldn't she?

Of course. Marnie must have kept it a secret from everyone. She'd certainly kept it a secret from Bobby.

"Time's up," a guard said, and only then did Luke look around to see that the room had emptied out, mostly.

Like a robot, he helped his father to his feet, shook Bobby's hand, listened to them promise to be in touch.

Bobby kept shaking his head, saying "Wow" and "I can't believe it."

Luke felt the same way.

"Send more pictures." Bobby's voice was choked up.

"That we'll have to discuss with Marnie's people." Dad looked at Luke, his eyes sharp. "You can do it, or I can."

"I'll talk to Hannah," he promised.

"Tell her—tell her I'd like to know them. If

that's possible." Bobby closed his eyes. "I've made so many mistakes."

"It could take time for them to adjust." Luke thought of how Hannah had seemed to withdraw whenever he mentioned Bobby. This wasn't going to be easy for her to accept. She was so moral, so upright, such a reputable member of the Bethlehem Springs community.

The thought of telling Hannah and her mother who the twins' father was…wow. Luke's neck felt hot and his stomach tightened. He thought he might lose his lunch.

And that had to pale beside what Bobby was going through. To find out, all of a sudden, that you were a father? Yeah.

"Talk to them as soon as you can, and let me know what they say," Bobby said.

"Yes," Luke said, "I will." In fact, he was going to go and see Hannah the moment he got home and got Dad settled.

He wanted—needed—to tell her the truth.

Chapter Fifteen

The knock on the door, late Saturday night, startled Hannah. When she saw a large shape outside, illuminated by the porch light, her heart started to pound as her mind darted to dozens of TV shows about intruders who broke in late at night.

A text pinged into her phone. It's me. Need to talk to you.

Luke. It was Luke! She jumped up and hurried toward the door, an involuntary smile creasing her face.

He'd been out of touch all day, even though she'd sent him a text letting him know that Mrs. Markowski had responded to their email. Her answer had been abrupt, but at least they knew she'd read it, was willing to talk and was considering letting Pinky be involved. Hannah had been concerned when Luke didn't answer, but she'd also been busy hosting a playdate for Addie and Emmy and cooking a big pot of lentil soup for dinner and for next week's lunches.

She went to the door, and her heart gave that big leap that was starting to happen every time she saw him. He was hatless, his hair unruly in the wind. Dark circles showed under his eyes. "Come in, it's cold," she said, opening the door.

He hesitated. "Can you come out? I'd like to talk privately."

He looked concerned, insecure, and she got a wild feeling that he was going to talk about them dating, about caring for her. What else would he want to be private about?

But that was ridiculous. She had to remember she wasn't the type of woman men like Luke made declarations to.

Although...wouldn't it be nice.

A gust of cold air caught the storm door, and she had to hold on tightly for a minute. It gave her the time to take a deep breath, and also, to realize just how cold it was outside. More of the dreaded wintry mix was predicted for tonight.

She needed to be hospitable and friendly toward Luke. No more, but no less, either. She beckoned him in. "Mom's upstairs watching TV, and the twins are asleep," she said. "It's pretty private in here, but I'll come out if you want."

"No. You're right, it's too cold." He came in,

shaking off a light coating of snow, and leaned down to unlace and take off his heavy boots.

When he'd stepped away from the boots, standing in the entryway in his stocking feet, he studied her, his forehead wrinkled. She couldn't interpret that expression, but it made her stomach turn over. "Your hair's wet. Sit down, and I'll make you some hot chocolate. How long have you been out?"

"I've been walking," he said, and went over to the couch.

In this weather? Why had he been walking?

She entered the kitchen and found some instant hot chocolate, wondering all the while what he was here for. If it was a minor work thing, he'd have told her by text, wouldn't he?

Unless he had another reason for being here.

Maybe even a romantic reason?

She stirred the hot-chocolate mix into two mugs of hot water. The aroma of it rose, homey and welcoming. She took the time to add a little coffee cream to it. He'd like that. She wanted to make him happy, although she didn't dare admit to herself why that was.

And she was delaying. Her hands shook a little as she carried out two mugs and set them down, carefully, on the coffee table. Then she sat at the other end of the couch from him. "So what's up?"

He took a sip of hot chocolate, put it down and turned to face her. "I have something to tell you," he said. "You may not like it, but bear with me."

Not a romantic visit then. She felt let down, which was absolutely ridiculous. "Okay," she said.

"It's hard to hear, but I wanted to tell you first thing."

She felt suddenly hot.

Steam rose from the cocoa. Sleet tapped against the windows as the wind made the old house creak. Lonely sounds, sounds that put them in a cold world of their own.

"We went to see Bobby today," he said.

Hannah's stomach dropped as if she'd just crested the hill on a roller coaster and was hurtling down. *Slow it down, delay, delay, he doesn't know.* Bobby didn't know, most likely, so Luke visiting him didn't have to have revealed anything.

He'll hate you when he finds out. The voice inside her head was authoritative, certain. He'd hate her because she'd kept the truth from him rather than telling him right away. "How is he?" she asked, hearing that her voice sounded high and silly.

"He's fine. Doing well, considering that he's in prison. But…" He hesitated.

"That's good he's doing well." It was hard for her to catch her breath.

She'd had to keep the secret. She'd made a promise to Marnie, for all kinds of reasons that had made all kinds of sense at one time.

"Yes. But between Bobby and Dad, we figured out…we'll have to do a DNA test to know for sure, but…" He leaned closer, that concerned expression on his face again. "There's no easy way to tell you. I think the twins—Marnie's twins, your nieces—are Bobby's."

He'd found out the truth. Before she could get up the nerve to tell him, he'd found out.

She sucked in a breath, staring at him. This was it.

He was going to hate her. Although, she suddenly realized, she could pretend not to know, could get herself off the hook. No one knew what Marnie had told her. She could act shocked.

But she was tired of secrets and concealing and hiding. And, anyway, she was bad at it. She'd never be able to pull it off.

But he would hate her.

She was still looking at him, trying to figure out what to say.

So she saw when his expression changed, saw him tilt his head to one side, saw the shock in his eyes. "You knew," he said. "You knew Bobby was the twins' father, and you didn't tell me."

* * *

Luke sat and stared at Hannah for what felt like a long time. Everything started to click into place.

She'd known. That was why she'd flipped out every time Bobby was mentioned. Not because she was such a moral, upright woman that the very thought of a felon horrified her, but because she'd lied to Luke.

Lied to him about those innocent little girls upstairs, who'd started to tug at his heart even before he knew…

Luke slammed down his cup of hot chocolate. It sloshed out onto the coffee table and dripped off the edge.

She didn't even look at it. "Luke, let me explain."

"No."

"I'm sorry," she said in a forlorn voice. "I'm so, so sorry."

Then, silence. A silence that felt extremely loud.

Luke didn't know how he got off the couch and into his boots and outside the house, though he did have a dim sense that he'd banged into the coffee table and sloshed more hot chocolate.

The trees bent and creaked in the wind. Underfoot, snow crunched.

The roaring, screaming wind echoed the feeling inside him.

She'd known the truth all along. She'd sat there with him and the twins, sat in the doctor's office and discussed their genetics with him beside her, and she still hadn't told him.

"Luke! Wait! Your coat." Hannah's voice rose above the wind and he realized that, yes, he'd forgotten his coat. Hadn't even noticed, because he was burning up.

She'd known the truth and kept it from him. Sweet, pure Hannah had flat-out lied.

He thought of his father's excitement, his brother's. They'd both been thrilled to discover that they were, respectively, the grandfather and father of two beautiful little girls.

And, yeah, they were both messed up. Bobby was *really* messed up. But they were human beings, and their feelings and rights had been discounted as if they were worthless. By the good Christian woman now calling his name from behind him.

A car's headlights flashed down the road just as Hannah caught up with him.

"Wait," she said, breathless. "This isn't safe. The road's icy. Come back and talk."

The car sped by, too fast for the conditions and too close. She was right. But he had to get away from her, had to move, had to walk.

She grabbed his arm. "At least put your coat on." She thrust it at him.

He took it. "Don't touch me," he said, pulling his arm away from her hand.

"Luke, I'm sorry," she said, her voice barely audible through the wind. "There were reasons I kept quiet. Marnie didn't want to…" She trailed off.

She was small and shivering, arms wrapped around herself. She wiped her nose with the back of her hand.

He stared at her as pellets of sleet nicked his face. "Did she give the girls Bobby's name?"

She shook her head. "She didn't list a father on their birth certificate," she said softly.

The reason was suddenly, blindingly obvious.

Marnie hadn't wanted to raise the twins with the stigma of being Hutchensons. And Hannah, by her silence, must have agreed with that decision.

It was a complete rejection of his family and of him.

Anger surged inside him, tightening every muscle in his body. He took a step toward her. "You lied." He took another step, and she backed away, her anguished expression turning into a simpler emotion: fear. "You knew this whole time, and you lied. Listened to my dad talk about how fortunate your mom was, being a grandmother, and didn't tell him that he was their grandfather."

"I know. It was wrong of me."

"You're a liar and a sneak," he yelled. Why try to control himself? He was a Hutchenson.

"Luke…" She reached out a hand, looked at his face and pulled it back. Stepped back.

She was scared of him. Well, she should be. "I thought you were better than your sister," he said, "but you're worse. At least she was up front about what kind of person she was. Not a hypocrite like you."

His fists clenched, and he turned around and started across the yard toward his father's place. But the thought of his dad, sick and excited, made him turn back. "You'll be hearing from us regarding our rights," he said. "Aside from that, I never want to see you again."

"But Luke…" Her eyes shone with tears. Crocodile tears. "We have to talk. We have to work together."

Yeah, because she needed his brawn to make her fancy training center for fancy people who fit into her fancy world.

People completely different from him, a Hutchenson. The fact that their families were linked, that those little girls upstairs in her darkened house were his nieces… The whole thing was just way too much.

"You're going to pay," he said. "Maybe starting with not getting that fantastic job you've been angling for. Explain that to your major donors." He spun and marched off through the sleety snow toward the house where he'd grown up, the house he didn't want to live in, but where he belonged.

He hated himself for listening, to hear if she kept after him, chased along. There was more yelling at her that he wanted to do, but she was silent.

When he got to the edge of the woods, he looked back. She stood there, staring after him, not saying a word. For the first time, he realized she wasn't wearing a coat herself.

"Go inside," he ordered, loud and rough.

She didn't move.

"Go on, go in."

"Luke..."

That pleading voice. He couldn't stand it anymore.

He turned and plunged into the woods toward the Hutchenson homestead, such as it was.

Chapter Sixteen

The Sunday morning after that awful Saturday night, Hannah sat in church alone, trying to pray.

People stood in the aisles chatting. Piano music played in the background, a medley of Christmas songs. The scent of evergreen branches and bayberry candles filled the air.

Hannah perceived it all through what felt like a fog. She'd seated herself in the back corner of the sanctuary because she didn't feel fit for human contact. Didn't feel entitled to it.

After a silent drive to church, her mother had swept the twins off to the nursery and stayed to help out there. She was furious at Hannah, who'd told her the truth early this morning.

Mom was right to be angry. Of all people, she was entitled to know the truth. Why hadn't Hannah at least trusted her mother with Marnie's secret, a secret that deeply affected the children she was helping to raise?

But I promised Marnie not to tell anyone, including Mom, because she knew Mom wouldn't keep it to herself.

The excuse felt hollow as soon as it came into her mind. Because when had she ever trusted Marnie's judgment over Mom's?

Thinking back, she saw all the mistakes she'd made. They were glaringly obvious. She shouldn't have agreed to keep Marnie's secret at all. Should have told Mom as soon as they'd gotten the twins home. Should have told Luke the first day she'd seen him back in town.

She'd been grief-stricken and confused and overwhelmed, but that wasn't an excuse for downright stupidity.

Gabby and Samantha were sitting side by side toward the front of the church, their husbands flanking them on the outside. As if she felt Hannah's gaze, Samantha turned and beckoned for Hannah to come join them.

She shook her head. She didn't feel like company, or like being that far toward the front of the church. And her friends loved her, but how would they feel if—when—they found out what she'd done?

Tonight, my place, Samantha mouthed to her. Their annual Christmas gift exchange was scheduled at Samantha's house this evening. She nodded. She wasn't sure she'd make it, but she didn't want to face questions right at this moment.

She breathed deeply, slowly, and closed her eyes. As the church quieted, a small shred of comfort penetrated her misery. Even now, God was here, was with her.

Please, Father, forgive me. Help me make it right.

When the music started, she opened her eyes and then blinked. Was that Luke, starting down the center aisle? With…his father?

There was an audible hush as the pair of them walked toward a seat in the middle. No one would say a word, but most people in town knew that Mr. Hutchenson hadn't darkened the door of a church, aside from the occasional wedding, in all his sixty-some years.

Luke didn't look from left to right, but his father did, almost as if he were searching for something. When he saw Hannah, he stood straighter and craned his neck as if to see whether Addie and Emmy were with her. When he realized they weren't, he spoke quietly to Luke. But Luke didn't look in her direction.

Another person she'd hurt. She'd deprived a sick man of the truth and his granddaughters.

Tears sprung to her eyes but she blinked them

back. As the service started, she tried to focus on it, to listen to the welcome and sing the opening hymn.

"And now," the pastor said, "we have a special treat from our kids." He gestured, and the Sunday school and older nursery kids filed in, most of them dressed in Christmas finery.

Please don't let the twins come in.

But, of course, in they came, along with a couple of other toddlers. They sat in front with the other children, each holding a drum or a bell.

Hannah leaned forward to see them better and inadvertently caught sight of Luke and his father. Both focused intently on the kids.

Why wouldn't they? They were seeing children they'd just realized were related to them.

The little song was sweet and the kids were adorable, most of them trying mightily to sing the words their teacher was mouthing to them. One little boy wandered over toward the preacher, who led him gently back. Another couple of girls waved vigorously to their families, not even trying to sing, making everyone chuckle.

If Hannah had been a better person she could enjoy it, but all she could think about was the salt it was rubbing in the Hutchenson men's wounds.

Finally, it was over. "And now, the children have a present for each of you," the head Sunday school teacher said. She gave baskets of small homemade Christmas ornaments to each child, and they walked around distributing them.

Hannah's mother was off to the side of the church, helping a little boy who used crutches, distributing his ornaments.

Addie and Emmy held hands and walked down the main aisle, each carrying a small basket that they held out to members of the congregation. Lots of "awwws" and "so sweets" ensued, for the twins in their matching red-and-green dresses, and for the other cute kids.

Then, right beside Luke and his father, Emmy stumbled and spilled her basket. Addie hurried to help, but the commotion upset Emmy, who started to cry.

Quickly, Hannah stood and sidled past the couple who'd sat down on the aisle end of her pew, her eyes on Emmy. She saw Luke's father reach out an arm, obviously trying to comfort the crying child, but she flinched away and cried louder.

Luke's father stared at the crying little girl for a long moment. Then he put his face in his hands.

Hannah rushed forward and picked up Emmy. She looked at Luke's father, whose head was still down, his shoulders shaking just a little.

Was he crying? He was crying. Of course, he was crying.

What would it feel like to know you had grandchildren, but be unable to connect with them? For them to be afraid of you? To have missed their early months and years?

Unsure of what to do, whom to comfort, Hannah turned to carry Emmy back to her seat, and then put a hand on Luke's father's shoulder, wishing she could do something.

Luke glared at her and gestured her away.

She obeyed the command, because what else could she do? She looked for Addie, but the child had gone over to Hannah's mom, who now stood holding her and watching the sad little tableau, her mouth in a hard, straight line.

"Let's get out of here, Dad." She heard Luke say the words behind her. By the time she reached her seat, he was helping his father down the aisle.

The old man's eyes were red, his shoulders stooped.

It had all taken place in a moment. Not many people had probably even noticed the little drama. Emmy's tears were soon dried, and she settled down with a baggie of stale animal crackers Hannah found in her purse.

Hannah didn't even try to pay attention to the rest of the service. Instead of church making things better, it—she—had made them worse. Not only was she not comforted, let alone forgiven, but she also felt like the most awful person in the universe.

Chapter Seventeen

"You made it!" Samantha opened the door and ushered in Hannah.

"Did I have a choice?" Hannah had tried to beg off when she'd spoken to her friends after church, but they'd insisted she come. Mom, softening, had said she was fine with keeping the twins, and that Hannah needed to spend time with Samantha and Gabby.

Mikey ran through the living room, brandishing an empty roll of wrapping paper as if it was a sword.

Corbin emerged from his study, took off his glasses and rubbed his eyes. "Sorry, sorry, I was supposed to have him out of here, and me, too." He wrapped an arm around Samantha, kissed the top of her head and then leaned down as if to kiss her more intently.

"You haven't even greeted our guests!" Samantha twisted away. "Hannah's here, and Gabby's on her way. I think…yes, that's her car out front. You men, scoot." She relented and kissed Corbin's cheek, then knelt down to hug Mikey. "Have fun and be good," she told him.

Gabby came in, and Corbin and Mikey left, and Samantha brought out a teapot and cups. "Grab that plate of cookies from the kitchen," she ordered Hannah.

They settled, Hannah and Samantha on the couch and Gabby on the easy chair that sat kitty-corner. Almost in unison, both of her friends rested their hands on their bellies and sighed.

"I can't wait for little miss Rachel to make her appearance," Gabby said. "Get this baby out of me!"

"Don't say that!" Samantha scolded. It was her first pregnancy, and she was cautious and worried about everything. "I'm so scared the baby will be premature." She and Corbin had elected not to learn the gender of their first child together, though Mikey, according to Samantha, prayed for a baby brother every night.

Hannah tried unsuccessfully to stifle the envy that wanted to rise up and smother her. Samantha and Gabby had loving husbands and babies on the way because they'd worked hard to make their marriages strong. They were good people.

They hadn't screwed up everything the way Hannah had.

"Have you heard from Sheniqua?" she asked, trying to make conversation and distract herself from her pain.

"I did." Gabby poured tea. "She said she and Ross's daughter are getting along great."

Sheniqua's mysterious relationship problems had turned into a holiday visit to her hometown, where she and an old neighbor-slash-boyfriend, now the single dad of a teenager, had patched things up and were apparently spending a lot of time together. "Amazing. Isn't his daughter fourteen or fifteen?"

"Uh-huh." Gabby took plastic wrap off the plate of red-and-white frosted Christmas cookies and passed them around. "Sheniqua spent all those years helping younger girls, including me. Now it's paying off for her."

"If this goes well, who knows? Maybe she'll come back with a ring on her finger."

"That would be so great." Hannah waved away the cookies. If Sheniqua got engaged, Hannah would be thrilled for her friend. Like the others, Sheniqua deserved happiness.

Sheniqua was also the last of Hannah's close girlfriends who was single.

"Sure you don't want cookies? You feeling

okay?" Samantha waved the plate under Hannah's nose.

"I'm fine. Not hungry."

Gabby and Samantha exchanged glances. "Tell us everything," Samantha ordered.

So Hannah did. Hesitantly at first, worried of what they'd think. But when she read sympathy and understanding in their eyes, the words poured out.

The gifts they'd brought—wrapped, used books, carefully selected to fit the recipient's interests—were forgotten. When Hannah finished, the other two were wide-eyed.

"So that's why Luke's dad broke down in church," Gabby said.

"Why he came in the first place," Samantha added. "Which…could be good, I guess."

Hannah shook her head. "I was awful. I hurt him so badly. Him, and Mom, and Luke." Her throat tightened on the last word.

"Oh, honey." Samantha leaned closer to give Hannah a quick hug. "It's too bad the way it happened, but don't blame yourself so hard. We all make mistakes."

"Besides," Gabby said, "it wasn't you who wanted to keep the secret. You promised Marnie."

"Marnie was an idiot." Hannah plunked down

her teacup with a clatter. "I should never have done what she asked."

Samantha, who'd known Marnie fairly well, tilted her head to one side. "She was kind of a mess, for sure."

"Sounds like it was more her fault than yours," Gabby said soothingly.

"Still, for you to hate and blame her only hurts you." Samantha took a delicate bite of cookie and then wiped her hands. "Corbin had a lot to forgive his father for, and his mom, too, but when he did, he was a whole lot easier to get along with."

"It's true. Hate will destroy you." Gabby bit her lip and looked into the fire, and Hannah glanced at Samantha. They both knew Gabby was thinking of Izzy's biological father, how his assault had led to Izzy's conception.

If Gabby could forgive that…

Hannah ignored the small, quiet voice inside. "I don't need to forgive Marnie that way," she said. "I don't hate her. I just…" She trailed off.

"What?" Samantha asked gently.

"I wish she hadn't screwed me up about men!"

Understanding came into Samantha's eyes. "Her boyfriend and what he did?"

Hannah nodded miserably. "And just when I thought I was getting past that…when I could kiss Luke and actually enjoy it…"

"You kissed Luke?" They both said it, loudly and practically in unison.

Hannah's cheeks heated. "Yeah. And yeah, it was great. But then Marnie's secret came out and everything hit the fan."

"Do you have any pictures of Marnie?" Gabby asked. "I never really knew her."

Hannah frowned. "Pictures? I might."

"In your phone?" Samantha asked. "I'd like to see them, too."

Why not? Hannah scrolled back in her phone. They hadn't taken pictures of Marnie's last hours; it had been the furthest thing from their minds. But that visit before, when they'd met the twins... There were a ton, and Hannah hadn't looked at them for a long time.

She pulled them up and her friends came to sit on either side of her. They oohed and aahed over the tiny twins, and exclaimed over how pretty Marnie was.

There was a picture of Hannah and Marnie, on the lawn in front of Marnie's apartment. Each of them had been holding a twin, and they were laughing hard.

Hannah couldn't remember the joke, but she could remember the feeling. Her big sister had been a natural comedian. They'd laughed together so many, many times.

"That's a beautiful picture." Samantha's voice caught a little.

"The two of you look a lot alike," Gabby said. "The same smiles."

Hannah's throat tightened.

"Do you think she was happy to have the twins?" Samantha asked.

Hannah thought back to that horrible, final day in the hospital. Marnie had been weak, barely able to hold up her head, but she'd gripped Hannah's hand so tightly it had hurt. "Take care of them like they were your own," she'd begged. "I've been an awful mother but you'll be…" She'd broken off, gasping for breath, and Hannah had reassured her through streaming tears that she would take care of them.

That was when Marnie had tugged Hannah closer, told her Bobby was the father and made her promise to keep the secret. "Bad enough they'll have my reputation," she'd said in a low, hoarse voice. "Can't be helped. You'll fix that. But I can't stand to think they'll grow up knowing their father's a—a murderer. Everyone will know. They'll be condemned…before they have a chance."

The beepers had started to go off. Marnie was so agitated. "Promise." She'd tightened her grip on Hannah's hand again.

Hannah had nodded, and Marnie had collapsed back. Not an hour later, she'd died.

"She loved them," Hannah choked out now, and then all the pain and hurt of losing her sister, hurt she'd hidden beneath righteous anger, came rushing out of her in a waterfall of tears.

"I can't stand that they'll never know her," she lamented. "They'll never know how funny she could be. They won't have a mother at their w-w-weddings!"

They all cried then, and Samantha rushed off to grab a big box of tissues. Long after her friends' sympathetic tears had dried, Hannah cried on.

It felt like her chest had been ripped wide open, leaving her heart exposed.

Hannah's beloved sister. The twins' mother.

Yes, Marnie had made mistakes, but who hadn't?

And if her loss was great, the twins' was so much greater. No mother to teach them the facts of life, to shop for prom dresses, to straighten their graduation caps. Yes, she and Mom would mother them as best they could, but it wouldn't be quite the same.

After a while, after more tissues and tea and hugs, they prayed together. Then, at Samantha's insistence, they opened their gifts to each other and exclaimed over their books.

Finally, as Gabby and Hannah stood to leave, Samantha frowned. "What about Luke?" she asked. "What are you going to do about him?"

"You need to talk to him." Gabby's voice was firm.

Hannah felt too emotionally drained to even attempt to figure that out. "We have to make a final push with Mrs. Markowski and Mr. Romano tomorrow. So we'll have to work together." She didn't know how, when he was so angry. But they had to try.

Chapter Eighteen

Monday morning, Luke pulled into the Rescue Haven parking lot right behind Mrs. Markowski's late-model SUV. He was pretty sure her appointment wasn't until ten, but here she was at 9:15 a.m.

When you could afford to drive a car like that, you got to call the shots.

As for Luke, he'd deliberately come in fifteen minutes late so he wouldn't have to watch Hannah take the twins into the Learn-and-Play. He'd watched the drop-off ritual countless times, had enjoyed seeing Addie's exuberance and Emmy's sleepy smile, but never before with the awareness that they were his nieces.

He just couldn't deal with that yet. He wanted to be in their lives, but for now, he couldn't bear to see Hannah walking along with them, as if she had the right, and the only right.

The times he'd been around Hannah and the girls played through his mind like a video on repeat: Thanksgiving, putting up Christmas decorations, taking Emmy to the doctor. As well as plenty of other casual moments in the yard or here at Rescue Haven.

Every one of those times, Hannah must have been aware that she was deceiving him, but she'd never let slip a word.

Instead, she'd made it seem like she actually cared for him, that for once he, Luke Hutchenson, might be enough.

But he wasn't enough, and his brother most certainly wasn't enough. She wanted to keep those precious little girls entirely separate from the tainted Hutchenson family.

Well, fine. He was staying away from them, too, at least this morning.

As he got out of the car, Hannah's car squealed into her usual parking spot, and Luke almost groaned.

Of course. He'd come late on purpose, to avoid her, on the very day she arrived late, as well.

If God had a sense of humor, Luke didn't find it very funny. He turned away, but Addie's rapturous "Luke! Luke!" pulled him back around.

She tugged away from Hannah and ran to him. Emmy followed more slowly, rubbing her eyes. For the life of him, he couldn't turn his back.

He knelt down and put out a hand to each girl, his throat going thick.

Emmy grabbed his fingers. Addie bypassed the extended hand and came in for a hug. He swallowed hard, smelling Addie's baby-shampoo hair, feeling Emmy's tiny hands clutching his.

He glanced up at Hannah and the sight of her pretty, deceptive face hardened him. He disentangled himself and stood.

"Come on, girls, time to go inside," he said. "Look, there's Miss Gabby!"

Easily distracted, the twins rushed to Gabby, who'd come outside with her own little girl, Izzy.

"Grandma!" Izzy crowed, and ran fearlessly over the slippery ground to Mrs. Markowski.

That sobered Luke. From what he understood, Mrs. Markowski's deceased son was Izzy's biological father, but the nonconsensual act that had conceived her… He didn't know the whole story, but he was pretty sure there had been a lot of crying and counseling before Mrs. Markowski and Gabby could greet each other cordially and dote together on little Izzy.

Only with God's help, and for the sake of a child, could that kind of healing take place.

As Gabby hurried back inside, ushering Izzy along with the twins, Mrs. Markowski brushed gloved hands together and turned to Luke. Lines formed between her weirdly dark eyebrows, and her red-lipstick mouth pursed. After glaring from him to Hannah and back again, she spoke. "I don't know what you have to show me that's so much better than last week. I have significant doubts that you can redeem yourself."

Hannah started earnestly expanding on the training plan they'd emailed to her. She helped Mrs. Markowski get her yapping poodle—was it wearing a *tutu*?—out of its crate.

Luke walked off to the side of the parking lot, trying to gather his mental resources. He wasn't sure how to get through this day. He'd tried praying, in that disastrous church service, but it hadn't gotten him very far.

Reese came to stand beside Luke. "I don't know what's up with you and Hannah," he said quietly, "but Gabby let me know you two are at odds. Whatever's going on personally, you need to get your head in the game."

Luke stared at the ground. "I'll try."

"The money generated by this new facility will help a lot of kids and a lot of dogs. And it'll probably determine your future here, as well as Hannah's. It's important."

"Got it." Luke turned away and marched over to the barn as Hannah and Mrs. Markowski tried to calm down the poodle. He would turn on the lights and heat, make sure the agility course was ready to go and then stay out of the way. Maybe he could get through today without letting down Reese and Rescue Haven, but also without having too much interaction with Hannah.

All too soon the two women came in with the dog. Hannah looked hassled. "Luke, could you move the jump height down?" she asked.

Yes, ma'am. He didn't look at her as he walked over to the jump and knelt to lower its height.

He felt something nudge his leg and realized the little poodle had come over. He reached out to scratch its ears.

"Don't!" Hannah and Mrs. Markowski both yelled.

Too late. The little dog sunk its teeth into Luke's hand.

He jerked away and ruefully studied the droplets of blood on his hand. He couldn't catch a break today.

The little dog backed off and stood growling at Luke.

"Pinky!" Hannah rushed over. "No biting. Luke, are you okay?"

"Yeah, but I'm steering clear of Cujo, here." He headed for the sink to wash off the blood. Not to be a wimp, but those little teeth hurt.

Mrs. Markowski intercepted him. "You shouldn't have touched Pinky. I don't appreciate that."

He stopped and studied her. Really, she wasn't

going to apologize for not keeping her brat of a dog under control? "I'll stay clear of her in the future." It was the nicest thing he could manage to say.

Behind him, he heard her muttering something about "there's not going to *be* a future."

Hannah soothed the woman and started instructing her in the basics of dog agility.

His role over for now, Luke headed for the farthest wall, whitewash can in hand. They'd decided to keep the rustic nature of the barn, rather than attempting to make it into a modern-looking facility. He got a stepladder, carried up his paint and started whitewashing the final wall.

The physical activity soothed him in about the same proportion that watching Hannah agitated him.

She was kneeling in front of the mouthy little dog. Just as she had with Goldie, she used treats to make it sit down, and then rewarded it, giving it some careful petting.

Mrs. Markowski stood beside Hannah and talked, probably spewing a constant stream of criticism, but Hannah didn't even look at her; her entire focus was on the dog.

Luke finished his section, moved the ladder and started another. And continued watching, because he couldn't help it.

Hannah was good at her job, he'd give her

that. She soon had the little monster wagging its tail and eating out of her hand.

Pretty much like Luke had done. She'd tamed him, too.

He'd wanted to help his father, do his duty and be a decent son, and then leave this town, where his name was a handicap.

Over the last few weeks, though, he'd started to see a different vision for his future.

Dad didn't just need help getting through surgery; he needed help getting through life. And he was changing. He'd actually been the one to suggest that he join Luke at church, and while a lot of that had been about catching a glimpse of his newly discovered granddaughters, Dad had paid attention to the readings, had even sung a little. To Luke's surprise, this wasn't Dad's first encounter with religion. He'd grown up attending church and was familiar enough to get by.

Still, there was no doubt that Dad would benefit from Luke's steadying influence.

He'd *thought* Hannah and the twins might benefit, too. More than that, he'd thought he needed Hannah. At least, for sure, he'd wanted her. He'd wondered if he was worthy, since she was so pure, but he'd started to catch a glimmer that maybe, just maybe, he could live up to—and find love with—a good woman like Hannah.

But that feeling was gone, swept away on the cold wind of her lies.

Pinky's yapping brought Luke's attention back to the present and the barn, and he realized he'd whitewashed over the same section of wall multiple times. As he climbed down to move his ladder, he saw that Hannah had hit a snag.

Pinky had apparently gotten afraid of the teeter-totter and was barking furiously at it as if it was a living thing. Hannah's soothing words and Mrs. Markowski's petting weren't enough to calm down the frantic dog. From this angle, Luke could see the problem: the teeter-totter was just a little off-kilter. Most likely, when Hannah had coaxed the dog to walk over it, it had banged down prematurely. Not only that, but it was also still a little high for the small poodle.

He shouldn't help Hannah; he should just let her crash and burn.

But like Reese had said, this was important and went beyond his own issues and problems with Hannah. A bunch of at-risk boys and dogs depended on Rescue Haven, and Rescue Haven depended on donors like Mrs. Markowski.

He looked around and located a wider, longer board. He carried it over, walking slowly.

Pinky's barking accelerated.

"Get away from her!" Mrs. Markowski's voice was shrill. "Can't you see she's upset?"

Hannah, though, saw immediately what he intended. "That would be perfect, but I don't know if the base can hold it."

"I'm the handyman, remember?" And why couldn't *he* remember that he was supposed to be mad at her?

He knelt in front of the teeter-totter and removed the small board. He made a couple of adjustments to the apparatus underneath and was able to fit the wider board on top and secure it.

"I don't see what good that will do." Mrs. Markowski had moved a few meters away and was holding Pinky, who had blessedly quieted down.

Hannah explained, her voice patient. "The longer board will make the angle more gradual, and the width of it will give her more security. Also, it looks different, so maybe she won't have that bad association with it. In fact..." She tapped a finger on her chin and looked around. "Luke, would you mind moving it to the other side of the enclosure? That way, she'll think it's a whole different thing."

He didn't mind, fool that he was. And he couldn't resist watching as Pinky approached the teeter-totter and then, lured by treats so strong Luke could smell them from where he stood, she walked up the slope.

Hannah held the board so that it didn't crash

down on the other side. She lowered it gently, still luring, and Pinky walked down with no fuss and looked expectantly at Hannah for her treat.

"That's a win!" Hannah crowed, taking a few steps backward and holding out a fist to bump with Luke's.

He turned away, walked away. That was how she sucked him in, and he couldn't let it happen again.

After Mrs. Markowski left, talking baby talk to Pinky the whole way, telling her what a smart dog she was, Hannah let out a sigh and flopped into a plastic chair.

"I think we're over the hump," she said to Luke, who was carrying a stepladder back to the storage area.

He didn't answer. Maybe he hadn't heard her. Coaxing Mrs. Markowski back into positivity about Rescue Haven and the new dog-training facility felt good. Forgiving Marnie, as she was starting to do, felt good.

Having the truth out about the twins, not having to keep the secret any longer—that felt good.

But being alienated from Luke was such a big barrier that it seemed to block out all the positive feelings.

When he walked back across the barn, she stood and walked toward him. "Thank you for being here for the center and for figuring out that teeter-totter problem," she said.

He kept walking toward the door. "It's my job," he said as he shrugged into his jacket.

She wanted to rush over to him, grab his arm and stop him from leaving. To ask if she'd see him before Christmas.

He opened the door, and cold air rushed in.

He was going to leave without saying anything more. And she wouldn't see him again. She took a few steps, hoping against hope that he'd turn back toward her.

He continued out, closing the door behind him.

Her chest hurt like someone had taken a knife and dug out her heart, leaving nothing but a raw, aching wound. She took a few more steps toward the door. She'd call him back, make him listen. Let him yell at her. Anything was better than this empty sense of loss.

Have some pride, she told herself.

Only she didn't have any pride. She ran to the door, opened it and rushed out into the blowing snow. "Luke!"

He stopped, half-turning. He didn't look at her.

"Do you—do you need any help with Goldie? The holidays might be a good time to work on training." What a stupid thing to say, when she wanted to bare her soul, but it was all she could think of.

"No, thanks. We're enrolling her in a class at Pet Express in January."

They'd replaced her that easily. She wouldn't even be able to work with Goldie again. A heavy feeling seemed to weigh down her eyes, her heart. And it was silly to feel sad about a dog, but Goldie wasn't just a dog. She had brought Hannah and Luke together, had been there, with her wagging tail and warm brown eyes, as they'd come to respect and care for each other.

Or at least, she'd thought they respected and cared for each other. With one mistake—admittedly a giant one, and all her fault—whatever they'd been building together had fallen apart.

She wanted to wail like a child, but she didn't want to burden him with her tears. She swallowed hard and looked at the ground. "Okay. Sure. Merry Christmas."

But when she looked up again, he was already gone.

Chapter Nineteen

The day after the successful session with Mrs. Markowski, which was also the first day of Rescue Haven's Christmas-week break, Luke intended to sleep in. But, of course, he'd woken up early, and at six thirty he'd given up the fight, dressed and gone downstairs to let out Goldie and grab some coffee. He made breakfast, and by seven thirty he was cleaning up and Dad was in his chair in the living room, watching TV.

There was a knock on the door.

Goldie, who now lived full-time in the house and felt it her job to defend it, barked wildly.

Hannah! His whole body surged with joy before he remembered he was furious at her, that she wasn't what she'd appeared to be, that she'd lied. That she hadn't wanted her family, her nieces, to have any connection with the horrible Hutchensons.

"You gonna get that, or do I have to?" Dad grumbled. He wasn't at his best in the morning, and he'd been especially moody since learning the truth about Bobby and processing the fact that Marnie hadn't even wanted to give Bobby's children the Hutchenson name.

Luke straightened his shoulders, walked over to the door in his stocking feet and opened it.

"Luke!" Addie's joyous voice greeted him, and he looked down and saw Emmy's shy smile.

But Hannah wasn't behind them—instead, it was her mother.

"We're here to see you, but mostly to see your father," she said briskly. "Can we come in?"

"Uh, we're still a little scruffy, but sure. Goldie, back up." He held the dog by the collar as Mrs. Antonicelli, Addie and Emmy came in.

"Who is it?" Dad called from his chair.

The girls ran toward the voice and the sound of the TV. Luke and Mrs. Antonicelli followed in time to see them start to approach Luke's father, then stop.

Dad clicked off the TV and leaned forward, smiling at the little girls. "Why, lookee here. It's Princess Addie and Princess Emmy."

That made the girls giggle.

"Where's your crowns, though?" He craned his neck, pretending to search.

Addie went to him and spun around. "No cwown."

"That's too bad," Dad said. "I bet your sister has one, though." He smiled at Emmy.

She shook her head and did her own slow twirl.

"Well," Dad said, "we'll have to find you girls some crowns."

Luke let Goldie go, figuring it would distract the twins from the fact that there were no crowns to be had. But he'd underestimated his father. As Goldie nuzzled the girls, making them giggle, Dad hauled himself out of the recliner and went over to the banister Hannah had helped decorate. He pulled off a piece of tinsel, used his pocketknife to cut it into two short lengths and twisted them into circles. Then he shuffled back to his chair and gestured to the girls. "Check it out, ladies, I found your crowns!"

As the girls rushed back to him, Luke realized his throat was tight. These were Bobby's girls, and Dad was already bonding with them.

"She told me Sunday morning," Mrs. Antonicelli said to Luke, her voice low. "I'm furious with her and Marnie, both. That was completely unacceptable, keeping the truth from you and your dad. Let alone from Bobby." Her voice had risen with indignation.

Dad must have heard her. He looked at them over the tinsel-crowned heads of Addie and Emmy. "I'm sure nobody was thinking real clearly right before Marnie passed."

"No, but it's been more than a month. Hannah had plenty of time and opportunity to tell all of us, especially you two."

"Oh, well." Dad picked up one of Goldie's toys and threw it across the room for the dog to fetch. As the little girls chased after Goldie, he gestured Mrs. Antonicelli in. "Come on, sit down. Luke, how about some coffee?"

So Luke went into the kitchen and made another pot of coffee while Dad and Hannah's mom talked in the living room and the girls chased Goldie around the house.

It was news to Luke that Hannah hadn't even told her mother. What was wrong with her? How could she have kept the truth from everyone, have participated in Thanksgiving and Christmas events with a smile on her face, while internally knowing she'd pulled one over on all of them?

She'd said she'd promised Marnie she'd keep the secret, but why had she done that? Hadn't she anticipated the problems that would cause?

That she'd be deceiving Luke and his father on a daily basis?

She didn't know you were in town, or that Dad was still living next door.

Okay, so she hadn't known it would be difficult to keep the secret. Still, she was supposed to be so moral, a good Christian. She hadn't been.

Again his conscience smote him. *You're a Christian, too. Aren't you supposed to forgive?*

Not lies like that! Not lies that stemmed from her hating the Hutchensons!

He carried the coffee out to the living room.

"We'll just go forward," Dad said as Luke put down the cups and turned back toward the kitchen for sugar and milk. "I'm the first to admit that I'm not the best influence, and Bobby's in prison. It's understandable that she didn't want us in the girls' lives."

Luke's steps slowed as shame overcame him. His father, for all his flaws, was behaving better than Luke was.

He sank down into a kitchen chair and let his head fall into his hands. When he thought of Hannah, his stomach churned with anger. Not just anger, but hurt.

Luke had worked hard to turn his life around, and he'd managed to do it. Hadn't Hannah seen that? Couldn't she at least have confided the truth to him? Didn't she think he was worthy?

Did she put him in the same category as his father and brother?

Was he different from them, really? Was he worthy?

He tried to pray, but the sound of the quiet conversation in the living room and the squealing girls running past him after Goldie made that hard. Still, he was able to empty his mind enough that some things from the Bible came to him.

He was no expert; he was just starting to study the New Testament more closely. But he knew the basics: everyone sinned and fell short.

Luke had turned his life around, but he was still a sinner. Right now, he was behaving considerably less Christlike than his father.

Hannah was a sinner, too. Maybe he'd put her on a pedestal before, thought she was too good for him, but it turned out she'd made a pretty big mistake, committed a big sin.

Did that mean she was unredeemable? Was he? Was Bobby or his father?

He felt someone nudging his leg and looked down. Emmy had come into the kitchen and sat down on the floor. She was leaning against him, looking up.

"Hey, honey," he said, immediately softening. "Did you get tired?"

She nodded and put her thumb in her mouth.

What was he supposed to do but pick her up and carry her out to her grandma? And how could he hold on to his unforgiving, hard stance with an innocent child in his arms?

After church on Christmas Eve, Hannah walked out of the sanctuary feeling emotional. She'd always loved Christmas Eve services, and this one had been as wonderful as usual. The candles, the carols, the beautiful readings... It was part of the family tradition and it stayed the same from year to year, providing a soothing regularity and a way to celebrate the central reality of their faith.

This year, there was more to celebrate and more to mourn. As she, Mom, and the twins joined the crowd milling around in the church's foyer after the service, as they accepted hot apple cider and Mom shared gingerbread boys from the bakery with all the children, Hannah didn't know how to feel. Joy for the twins, their sweetness and cuteness. Pleasure for her mom, who was in her element, distributing cookies and accepting compliments about her granddaughters.

Sadness that Marnie wasn't here to see it. Of course, she hadn't been in town for the holidays for a couple of years. But when they'd been younger, Marnie had been beside Hannah in church, usually making Hannah laugh with some inappropriate remark about someone's Christmas outfit or out-of-tune singing. As kids, they'd shared the excitement of knowing there were presents under the tree. She, Mom and Marnie had been a family, bonded even more tightly after Dad had died when they were so young.

Now, their family had suffered another loss. They'd gained the twins and lost Marnie. Would they bond more tightly or let the issues push them apart?

Luke and his father emerged from the sanctuary and walked through the crowd. Luke glanced her way and then steered his father in the opposite direction. That was no surprise, nothing more than she deserved. She was glad to see that the congregation was welcoming Mr. Hutchenson, who was a little more scraggly-looking than most of the men, dressed as he was in a work shirt and jeans. His beard didn't look as wild as usual, though, and Hannah wondered whether that was his idea or Luke's.

She wanted to know. She wanted to talk to him about the services and the twins and Rescue Haven. Wanted to share a laugh about the kid who'd jumped up in the middle of the service to ask the pastor where the presents were.

It wasn't going to happen. She sank down

onto a couch in the corner by herself, trying not to cry.

Then, suddenly, it was as if she could see herself from the outside. She was acting like a whiny child, a dishrag. If she wanted things to be better with Luke, if she wanted to at least regain his friendship, she couldn't expect that to happen by sitting in a corner.

And, yes, he'd probably shoot her down, but at least she could go to sleep tonight knowing she'd tried.

Before she could lose what little courage she had, she stood and walked toward the thinning crowd. Had they already left?

But no; there was Luke helping his dad into his heavy winter coat. She hurried over. "Can I talk to you a minute?"

"We were just leaving." Luke's voice was cool, and Hannah's courage flagged.

"It won't take long."

He sighed. "What is it?"

Mom's voice came from behind her. "I'm taking the twins home, and I can easily give you a ride if you'd like, Stan."

Even in the midst of her discomfort, Hannah looked at her mother in surprise. *Stan?*

Her mother lifted her chin, avoiding Hannah's eyes. "That's if your son can bring my daughter home." She turned to Luke. "Can you?"

No doubt Luke would have said no if it was Hannah asking, but she saw in his face that he couldn't turn down her mom. "Sure," he said, his voice anything but enthusiastic.

There was a bustle of getting the twins into their coats, and then Hannah and Luke walked everyone out, to discover that a light snow was falling.

"Are you sure you're okay to drive home, Mom?"

Her mother rolled her eyes. "I've been driving in this weather since I was sixteen. I think I can handle a dusting of new snow."

Finally, everyone was in the car. Addie bounced with excitement while Emmy looked ready to nod off in her car seat.

Hannah had a cowardly urge to climb in between the girls, but she stood up to it. She closed the car door and watched as Mom drove the little group away.

Now it was just her and Luke.

The parking lot was emptying, the pastor waving from the doorway. "I'm guessing he wants to go home, too," Luke said, the implication being that he wanted to get home, as well. "What did you want to say?"

Hannah shivered and wrapped her coat more tightly around herself. Where to begin?

He sighed. "Do you want to get into my car, where it's warm?"

But she didn't want to be enclosed like that. She needed the comfort of God's beautiful creation around her. "Can we walk a little?"

"Are you dressed for it?" His gaze swept over her dress coat and boots, and then he looked away.

"I'm fine. There's a little path toward town."

She gestured toward the pines that lined the edge of the church property. An opening between them led to a little curved bridge over a brook. It led to the town park, and was known as a sort of lovers' lane.

Luke wasn't going to make this easy, but she had to speak her piece. Had to not only apologize, but also…well. She would see how far her courage would go.

Tell him.

But I'm not the kind of woman who succeeds with relationships, she argued with herself.

Tell him.

But being forward, dressing pretty, being girly… That leads to disaster.

Only it wouldn't, not with Luke. He was a good man. Such a good man. And for the sake of the girls, for her own sake, she had to try.

The snow drifted down, twinkling and sparkling. Clouds scudded across the dark sky, and in a few spots, stars were visible.

Behind them, a car door closed. A motor started up, and then the car drove off.

It was quiet.

They walked toward the park. Hannah's heart pounded so hard she felt like she was going to explode.

She should just start small, with an apology.

Only, she reminded herself, the apology was really the big thing. It was what would make a friendship possible, and that was crucial for the twins.

She stole a glance at Luke. His coat was open, his head bare. On his face she could see the heavy stubble that meant he hadn't had time to shave.

He didn't look angry, exactly, but he also didn't look friendly.

"Luke," she said, "I'm sorry for what I did. With all my heart, I apologize. I was wrong to keep Marnie's secret, and I hurt a lot of people. Your dad, my mom, the twins…and you."

He didn't look at her; he looked at the snowy path in front of them. What did that mean?

Her foot slipped on an icy patch.

He caught her arm. "Careful," he said. He steadied her and let go.

Her heart melted a little, because that was Luke. Protective, even when he was angry.

"I'd like to work to make it up to you," she said, plowing on. "Help you all to build relationships with Addie and Emmy."

"That would be…good." He glanced over at her. "We all make mistakes, Hannah. I get that."

It was a softening of his attitude, and she almost sagged with relief. "Do you forgive me?" she asked, needing reassurance.

He drew in a deep breath and for a scary moment, he didn't speak. Then he looked at her and nodded. "I forgive you."

A weight lifted from her heart. Luke wouldn't say he forgave her unless he meant it. If that was all she could have from him, it was a wonderful blessing.

But she'd promised herself she'd go all the way, say it all. "Thank you. I appreciate that. But…there's more."

They were approaching a little bridge that arched over a stream. The boards were slippery, and he took her arm. "Be careful, slow down and tell me everything, kiddo," he said, reverting to a name she remembered from their childhood.

She swallowed, grateful for his gentler tone, but wondering if he saw her as a kid still. Probably, sometimes.

Not when he'd kissed her, though.

Just say it.

"The thing is, Luke, I've..." She sucked in a convulsive breath. "I've kind of fallen in love with you."

There. It was out. Relief warred with terror in her churning gut.

He didn't speak, but slowed as they reached the highest point on the little bridge. He let go of her arm, stopped and looked down at the snowy creek, the sound of its water bright beneath the snow and ice.

His face was as still as stone.

She'd hoped for a different reaction. *But,* she reminded herself, *he's a good man. He won't hurt me. He'll let me down easy.*

"I mean it, Luke," she said, pushing on. "I love you for your caring and your sense of humor and the way you'll help me out even when you're mad."

Something quirked the side of his mouth. Maybe it was a smile, or the start of one.

"I think maybe... Maybe I've loved you since I was a little girl scared in a barn with a bunch of kittens," she said.

He looked at her then. "Big-brother stuff."

"No," she said quickly. He was getting the wrong idea. She was bad at this, obviously. "I mean, maybe a little, but I think you're really handsome. And—" In for a penny, in for a pound. She sucked in a shaky breath. "I loved kissing you. Look, I know you're charismatic and good-looking and sophisticated, way out of my league. I'm not expecting you to respond in kind. I just wanted you to know."

There. She'd said her piece, made a fool of herself, and her emotions were churning. She thought she might cry or be sick. No doubt it was the worst declaration of love in the history of Bethlehem Springs. But it was out.

It was only fair that she be the one to put herself out on a limb, since she was the one who'd made a mess of things. Plain she might be, but she hoped he could see that she was honest, and trying.

And he hadn't spoken, other than the big-brother thing. Hadn't looked at her, but just continued to stare off into the icy stream, covered over by a lacework of bare branches. What was going through his mind?

Luke tried to get his feelings under control, tried to use the icy surroundings to cool himself down, but the truth was, he was burning up. What had just happened? It was like he couldn't take it in.

He turned his head and looked at this woman who didn't know how beautiful she was. Yes, she'd done wrong. So had he, many times, big and small.

That awful day when Nicki had waved back at him from her mother's car window, not knowing she'd never see him again... That day, that mess of mistakes, came to mind. That was the worst, but there were so many others. His rabble-rousing here in town, his fights with his father, his neglect of his brother.

But she'd said she thought him a good man. That she liked kissing him.

She considered *him* out of *her* league. Wow. That was so ridiculous he almost laughed.

He'd thought, fleetingly over the last few weeks, that if things were different he'd want to pursue a relationship with her, something serious. If he hadn't been a Hutchenson. But maybe...

He faced her then, took her arm and turned her so she was facing him. He reached out and, with one careful finger, pushed back a lock of her hair. "You're brave and you're beautiful."

She looked away. "I don't think I'm either of those things."

"Ah." He touched her cheek and got her to look at him again. "Taking on a gruff old bear like me, that's brave."

"You *have* been kind of gruff the last few days," she ventured.

"And, Hannah." He let his eyes flicker down to her lips. "I loved kissing you, too. More than anything."

"You did?" She looked so vulnerable that he couldn't resist dropping a kiss on her cold lips. Which was dangerous, because then he wanted to pull her close and go on kissing her all night. So he kept it short and sweet, and still his heart pounded like a heavy bass drum as he backed up a little and took both of her hands in his.

"Well," she said, a little breathlessly, "I'm glad we've established that the kissing is good."

"It's more than that. I care for you, Hannah. A lot."

Her eyes widened as she stared at him. "Really, Luke?"

He tried to think how to put his feelings into words. "Really. I admire you, the way you took on Addie and Emmy without hesitation. The way you helped Goldie and that rotten little Pinky."

Her mouth quirked into a tiny smile. "She is awful, isn't she? How's your hand?"

"Fine. I love how cute you are, just like when you were a kid, and how beautiful you are as a woman."

She looked down, a pink flush crossing her cheeks. "I'm not."

"You don't even know it, and that's better than

being full of yourself, but... I'd be happy to keep reminding you."

Overhead, the clouds shifted and a ray of moonlight lit their surroundings, with the creek, the path and the church steeple visible in the distance.

She looked flushed and stunned and confused.

"So..." He took a deep breath. "Do you think we should...see each other? Give it a go, see if we can build something together?"

Her troubled eyes met his, then looked away. "Do you mean it, Luke? You're not just saying it to be nice?"

He laughed, because her reaction was so Hannah. "No, silly girl. I'm saying it because I'm crazy about you."

She looked at him and it was like the stars shone out of her eyes. Then she lifted her face and walked into his arms.

Holding her was the best thing Luke had ever felt. He wanted like anything to propose, to seal the deal. But there was a part of him that was holding back.

Was he really good enough for someone as wonderful as Hannah?

The sun was just rising in a swirl of pink and gold clouds when Luke and his father knocked on the Antonicellis' door.

It was Christmas morning. Luke had spent most of the night thinking about Hannah, what she'd said, how it had felt to hold her in his arms.

Although they'd talked about exploring a relationship, he was sure she wasn't expecting to start so soon. Would she be glad to see him today, or was it too much?

But Dad had arranged it with Hannah's mom, that they'd come over early, in time to see the twins' first Christmas here in Bethlehem Springs. Dad had gone overboard buying gifts, and truth to tell, Luke had, too; in fact, they'd brought the car because there were too many packages to carry.

Luke couldn't tell Dad they should wait until later in the day, not when there was so much joy in his eyes. Being a grandpa was going to be good for him.

Hannah's mom opened the door and beckoned them in. "Come in, come in out of the cold," she said, smiling. "I'm just putting together some breakfast before the girls wake up." She stepped back and held the door for them. "Oh, my, you men brought so many gifts! You didn't need to do that."

"I just learned I'm a grandpa a week ago, Alice," Dad said. "You can't blame me for wanting to spoil them."

There was something about the way his father

was looking at Hannah's mom. Luke took a step back and watched as the two of them arranged the gifts around the lopsided Christmas tree, its ornaments clustered mostly around the bottom third of it. Twin height, he realized.

One by one, Dad handed their clumsily wrapped gifts to Hannah's mom. At one point, their hands touched in the exchange and their eyes met for a fraction longer than was usual between neighbors. It happened again a moment later.

Wow.

Addie's loud chortle came from upstairs, followed by Hannah's laugh.

In the spirit of helping his father along, Luke spoke up. "Dad, why don't you stay down here and help with breakfast while Hannah and I get the girls up? If that's okay," he added, looking at Hannah's mom.

She smiled at him, her cheeks dimpling. "Perfectly okay."

Luke trotted up the stairs, and what he saw through the half-open door took his breath away.

The twins sat on a little bed, side by side, dressed in bright Christmas pajamas: red for Addie, green for Emmy. Their blond hair was tousled, curls tumbling over their round faces. Hannah sang a silly song about Christmas, tickling their toes through their footie pajamas, making them laugh.

As for Hannah, she wore snug faded jeans, a red sweater and big fluffy slippers. If he had to guess, he'd say she hadn't even combed her hair. Definitely no makeup.

She looked gorgeous.

And she'd said last night that she cared for him. That she'd fallen in love with him. This could be his family.

But you're a Hutchenson.

Hannah looked up and saw him, and blushed. "Why didn't you tell me you were there! I'd have stopped my bad singing!"

"Luke!" Addie cried, holding out her arms.

"*Uncle* Luke," Hannah corrected.

"Unca Luke." Emmy said it almost thoughtfully, studying him with big blue eyes.

His heart full, he walked into the girls' bedroom then, patted Emmy's leg, picked up Addie and swung her until she squealed with laughter. "I got sent up to help," he said to Hannah as he landed Addie safely back by her sister's side. "Or rather, I volunteered. I got the feeling Dad and your mom could use a little privacy."

She raised an eyebrow. "I got the same feeling last night. She called him Stan."

They worked together to comb the girls' hair and brush their teeth. In the midst of it all, in between admiring how pretty Hannah was and how well she did the mothering tasks she'd only recently undertaken, Luke's mind raced.

He'd instantly decided to support his dad in pursuing Hannah's mom. But Luke's dad was more of a Hutchenson, with all that entailed, than Luke was.

Luke was being more generous and forgiving with his father than with himself.

They carried the girls downstairs. A cinnamon scent wafted through the air as the girls ripped at their gifts, clumsily, seeming as interested in the ribbons and paper as in the toys and outfits inside. Dad sat on the couch, beside Hannah's mom, with a small but respectable space between them.

Hannah seemed to be everywhere, scrambling around on the floor to distribute the packages, helping Emmy with one that was wrapped too tightly, stopping Addie from putting a pretend potato from her new plastic food set into her mouth. She was so agile in her movements, so patient in her dealings with the girls, so quick to smile and laugh.

So beautiful.

When the girls started to get overwhelmed with their many gifts, Hannah helped them carry presents to her mom and his dad: plaster handprint ornaments on ribbons, red for Addie's, bright purple for Emmy's.

Dad got too choked up to thank them, but when Emmy held out her arms, he pulled her into his lap and hugged her gently. Addie climbed into Hannah's mom's lap and told her, excitedly, how they'd made the ornaments as a secret surprise.

Hannah watched and wiped a tear. Luke's own throat felt a little tight.

Hannah cared for him. This could be his family. But did he deserve it?

He looked at the crèche then, displayed on the hearth. Gaudy plastic figures, safe for the girls, but it was what it symbolized that mattered.

Luke had made plenty of mistakes. So had his father, for sure. His brother was practically the king of mistakes, and if he was the king, Marnie was the queen. Even Hannah, such a good person, had made a big mistake.

But through the baby born on Christmas, they were all forgiven, made as innocent as these little ones now playing on the couch between their grandparents.

Suddenly, he couldn't wait another minute. "Want to come walk Goldie with me?" he asked Hannah. They'd left the dog at home, knowing the morning's activities would be too chaotic for her.

Hannah tilted her head to one side, eyes curious. "Um, sure, if it's okay with everyone."

"Do it," her mom said.

"I'd grab any chance to play with these little sweethearts." Dad tickled Emmy's hand with the tip of his finger, and she smiled and leaned against his side.

Luke and Hannah went out into the bright Christmas sunshine and walked through the woods to his house, making the first footprints on the pristine snow. Goldie was ecstatic to be let out. She bounded around the now-fenced backyard, ears flopping, sniffing at deer tracks, barking at a bold squirrel.

Luke snapped a leash on her, and they took a snowy path that ran back behind their houses through the woods and fields. The crisp air felt good to Luke, who was a little overheated.

They'd agreed to take their friendship to a new level, but what would that entail? Despite all his experience with women, Luke felt as awkward as a high-school boy on his first date.

But there was no use giving in to fear, so he plunged in. "I've been thinking about what you said last night."

"Yeah?" She glanced up at him, eyes wide, maybe a little insecure.

"Yeah. Look, I'm a Hutchenson. That carries a stigma in this town."

He figured she'd reassure him, because that was her nature. But she didn't. Instead, she took Goldie's leash from his hand. "Goldie, sit," she said.

Goldie sat instantly in the snow, tail wagging.

Luke was confused, and a little worried. Why wasn't she answering?

"Down," Hannah said, and Goldie lay down.

Was she trying to avoid a serious discussion? Had her feelings about him already changed?

"Stay," she commanded the panting dog. She dropped the leash and backed away.

Goldie stayed, watching Hannah intently.

Luke was watching her, too, increasingly concerned about the way she was ignoring him.

"Okay, good girl, come!" Hannah pulled a treat from her jacket pocket—apparently dog trainers always carried them—and fed Goldie, then praised her extravagantly.

Then she looked at Luke. "Goldie's a Hutchenson," she said, "and look how far she's come."

"Look how far…" And then, when he got it, Luke threw back his head and laughed. "Oh, Hannah," he said. "I don't want to wait."

She stopped patting and rubbing Goldie and tilted her head to one side, studying him. "What does that mean?"

This was the moment. *Go for it.* "It means," he said, "I want you to be my wife."

She blinked, and a funny little sound came from her throat.

"I know it's soon, and we said we'd just try all this out." He gestured from his own chest to her and back again. Now that he'd started, he had to convince her. "But I want to be with you every day, to help raise the girls, to have Dad and your mom close by. I want a family, a good family, and I want it now, not later. With God's help, we can make it work. I know we can."

She bit her lip, and then the biggest smile broke across her face. "Oh, Luke…" She sucked in a breath. "Wow. I just…" She hesitated, and then spoke in a rush. "I can't believe a girl like me could be married to someone as cool as you."

That made him laugh. "I'm far from cool. In fact, I'm sweating." Because she hadn't really answered him.

"You *are* cool," she insisted, "and handsome, and kind, and hardworking. And fun, fun to be with."

"Then…" He realized what he'd left out, and sank to his knees. "Will you marry me?"

Both hands flew to her mouth and her eyes got shiny. And then she grasped his hands in her gloved ones. "Nothing could make me happier."

Fireworks started going off inside him, but it felt too easy. "You know it's because I love you, right?" He squeezed her hands. "Because you're warm and beautiful and good, and I just want to hold you forever."

She opened her arms, a little like Addie, and he stood and pulled her close and kissed her.

Later, they headed back toward her house, holding hands, Goldie trotting alongside them.

"We can wait if you want," Luke began, making himself say the words. "Have a real, long courtship, like you deserve."

She looked at him sideways through those long eyelashes. "Actually," she said, "I'm ready anytime. As soon as possible." She paused, then added, "Actually, I can't wait."

He felt like pumping his fist and shouting to the skies, but instead, he put an arm around her and pulled her close to his side. "I'll get you whatever kind of ring you want," he said. "You deserve diamonds. Way more than diamonds."

"Oh, Luke." She turned into his arms, and it was way, way more than *he* deserved, this woman, this joy that filled his heart to bursting.

He shut his eyes, clasped his wife-to-be close and, in his heart, whispered a Christmas prayer of thanks.

Epilogue

⟨◦⟩

They did marry soon, in fact, on Valentine's Day, in the most romantic and wonderful wedding Hannah had ever experienced. It was simple, because she and Luke were simple, but it was perfect.

Luke's father was still rough around the edges and always would be. But he was healing from his surgery, and his strong desire to be sober for Addie and Emmy had improved his lifestyle. To Hannah's surprise, the girls adored him, and he'd made a special connection with quiet Emmy.

Addie was Luke's girl—when he threw her up in the air she screamed with delight, and she was always jumping into his arms—although Hannah truly couldn't say that he favored one girl over the other. Their hands were full, but with the support of their community, they were able to do it all and still have time for romantic nights in front of the fire or walking in the woods. They'd moved temporarily into Hannah's old house, but were planning to buy the property just across the street from Mom's so that the girls could grow up close to both their grandparents.

And now, three months after the wedding, they were taking the twins to see Bobby for the first time.

The guard led them to a grassy area with a couple of plain benches, surrounded by a high chain-link fence with barbed wire at the top. Hannah had a moment of misgiving when she saw that. Was it right to expose the girls to Bobby?

Luke, seeming to read her mind, put a reassuring arm around her shoulders. "They'll be fine."

She nodded, closed her eyes and seemed to see Marnie's face. How many times had her big sister laughed at her fears?

She remembered that last hour of Marnie's life, too, and the promise she was breaking. *I'm sorry*, she whispered internally, just to Marnie. *But Luke's here, and Mom, and their grandpa, and I think it's gonna be okay.*

Her heart ached a little. If only Marnie could have beaten her addiction and come back home, she, too, could have been surrounded by love and support as she raised her girls.

"There he is." It was Mr. Hutchenson's voice, and Hannah opened her eyes to see Bobby.

The expression on Bobby's face, as he saw his children in person for the first time, was priceless, and it told Hannah, for sure, that they were doing the right thing. He pressed his hands to his mouth and walked a little closer, then sank down on his knees—either to make himself smaller and less intimidating, or because his legs wouldn't support him, Hannah wasn't sure which.

Addie tugged Hannah's hand. "My daddy?"

Hannah's throat tightened. "That's right, sweet pea. That's your daddy."

Addie nodded. The twins had grown so much in the past few months, but Addie was still the leader. She took Emmy's hand, and slowly, they walked to Bobby.

Hannah reached blindly for Luke, her vision blurring, and he put his arm around her. When she looked up at him, she saw that his eyes were brimming over, too.

She heard a sob behind her—Mom—and reached back a hand, and Mom came forward, Mr. Hutchenson on her other side.

And they watched as two little girls and one flawed, repentant man became a family.

There were hugs afterward, and more tears and even some laughter, and the visit was all too short. Exhausting, too. In the car on the way home, the twins, Mom and Mr. Hutchenson fell asleep.

Hannah reached out and put an arm around her husband, touched the back of his neck.

He smiled over at her briefly before his eyes went back to the road. "Do you think it was the right thing to do?"

"I do," she said. "Almost as right as marrying you."

She took his hand and kissed it.

"Hey now, that's not very nice of you to start something I can't finish because I'm driving," he groused playfully.

She squeezed his hand. "We'll finish later," she said, her heart brimming with thanks and love. "We have the rest of our lives."

* * * * *

Dear Reader,

Thank you for reading the third novel in my Rescue Haven series. I love stories about overcoming the past, so writing about Luke and Hannah felt natural to me. Luke learns that he's not defined by his family's reputation and difficult history, and Hannah realizes she doesn't have to miss out on love because a teenage incident made her uncomfortable with dating.

We all struggle with something from the past. But just like Luke, we can embrace Christ's love and the sacrifice He made for us. We can be healed, and Christmas is a wonderful time to reflect on that beautiful reality.

Do you like "seasoned" romance? You may have noticed that after they become grandparents together, Luke's father and Hannah's mother started to develop feelings for each other. If you'd like to see how their story turns out, visit my website and sign up for my newsletter, and you'll gain access to their short and sweet romance. It's a small holiday gift to you, my wonderful readers.

Merry Christmas to all!
Lee

Get 4 FREE REWARDS!

We'll send you 2 FREE Books <u>plus</u> 2 FREE Mystery Gifts.

Love Inspired books feature uplifting stories where faith helps guide you through life's challenges and discover the promise of a new beginning.

FREE
Value Over
$20